DO
THE REIGN OF TERROR

DOCTOR WHO
THE REIGN OF TERROR

Based on the BBC television series by Dennis Spooner by
arrangement with the British Broadcasting Corporation

IAN MARTER

Number 119 in the
Doctor Who Library

TARGET

A TARGET BOOK

published by
the Paperback Division of
W.H. ALLEN & Co. PLC

A Target Book
Published in 1987
By the Paperback Division of
W.H. Allen & Co. PLC
44 Hill Street, London W1X 8LB

First published in Great Britain by
W.H. Allen & Co. PLC 1987

The BBC producers of The Reign of Terror were Verity Lambert
and Mervyn Pinfield, the director was Henrick Hirsch
The role of the Doctor
was played by William Hartnell

Printed and bound in Great Britain by
Anchor Brendon Ltd, Tiptree, Essex

ISBN-0-426-20264-3

CONTENTS

1

So Near And So Far

The twilit forest was hot and muggy. Not a breath of air stirred the motionless trees and the invisible creatures were ominously silent, as if they were waiting for some cataclysmic storm to erupt around them. There was an electric menace in the humid stillness and the trees hung like dormant monsters awaiting their hour to spring to life and stalk across the land in reawakened and invincible majesty. For the land was troubled. Majesty had been abolished and an unnamable terror lurked everywhere.

Without warning, leaves suddenly shivered and branches creaked and swayed. In the thickly clustering undergrowth, twigs broke off and flew in all directions as the foliage whipped back and forth, and leaves were sucked in a violent swirling vortex into the air. The tall shadows were filled with a harsh grinding wail, as if some vast primitive being were in torment. A dark alien shape thrust the branches aside and flattened the mossy ground like a giant foot, growling and rumbling as it gradually solidified. Its great winking yellow eye gave a final malevolent glare and went dark. Its tormented roars subsided. The flying leaves and shattered twigs fluttered to the ground as the tortured foliage ceased its lashing struggle.

The forest held its breath as if listening and watching to see what the alien intruder would do. But for a long time it did nothing at all. It was a blue-painted wooden structure, rather like a fat sentry box. On its roof was an amber-coloured beacon and around the top sat a row of frosted glass

7

windows. Above the windows on each side was a neatly painted notice announcing that it was a:

POLICE PUBLIC CALL BOX

Another notice on a metal panel beside the main door explained how the public could use the telephone behind the panel to contact the emergency services.

In the humid shadows the object looked completely out of place. It was also completely out of its time . . .

Inside the police box four people were standing around a large hexagonal console which was covered in dials, displays, gauges, buttons, levers and other highly advanced instruments. In the centre of the console, a transparent cylindrical mechanism which had been slowly spinning to and fro and rising and falling was just settling to rest, watched intently by the four onlookers.

Around them, the chamber, which was about the size of a large high-ceilinged room, hummed and murmured like some giant electronic beast. Its white walls were composed of cellular panels, each with a central hole. Apart from the console in the middle, the chamber was bare except for odd items of bric-à-brac, like an ancient brass astrolabe and a rickety wooden armchair drawn up to the controls.

A severe-looking old man bent over the console, frowning as he tinkered with buttons and switches. His long silver hair was brushed straight back from his lined and hollow-cheeked face and his mouth was compressed in a thin strip which turned down at the ends in a kind of grimace of permanent disapproval. His sharp grey eyes gleamed with vigilant attention, peering down his beak-like nose at the array of instruments under his bony fingers. The old man was dressed in a short black frock-coat, a white shirt with wing collar and narrow cravat tied in a large untidy bow, a striped waistcoat and baggy checked trousers slightly too short for him.

With an irritable grunt he straightened up, threw back his large head and stared at his three younger companions, his nostrils flaring impatiently. 'There you are then. England.

8

Home!' he snapped, twisting a large ring round and round on the middle finger of his right hand.

A tall dark-haired woman of about twenty-eight wearing a full-skirted sleeveless dress tightly belted round her slim waist put her hand on the old man's arm. 'Doctor, we really do appreciate all you've . . . '

The old man waved her aside. 'Quite, Barbara. Young Chesterton here has made your position perfectly clear . . . ' he said coldly, gesturing at the young man who was standing beside her with his hand on the shoulder of a girl of sixteen with huge sad eyes. 'And now, if you'll excuse me, I have work to do.'

The young girl clutched anxiously at his sleeve, her lips trembling and her brown eyes glistening with tears. 'But Grandfather . . . '

The Doctor shook his head firmly. 'Now, now, Susan. Say your goodbyes to Ian and Barbara. We must leave immediately,' he insisted.

Susan turned to Barbara and hugged her like a child embracing its mother. In her white shirt, gymslip style dress and white ankle socks she suddenly looked vulnerable and lost, despite the hints of a maturity beyond her years in the pale round face framed with short dark hair.

Catching Barbara's pleading glance, Ian Chesterton stepped in front of the Doctor as the old man moved round the console muttering mysteriously to himself about co-ordinate tolerances and quantum conjugation vectors. 'Doctor, do you always have to be in such a tearing hurry?' he protested resentfully. Ian was a little older than Barbara Wright. His cheerful, regular features and neatly parted black hair gave him an air of honest reliability and he had often been described as 'open-faced'. In his dark round-necked sweater and flannels he appeared exactly what he was – a schoolteacher like Barbara.

The Doctor ignored him for a moment and fiddled with his instruments. 'Time enough has been wasted already in bringing you back to Earth, Chesterton,' he eventually retorted. '*I* have the Universe to explore.'

Ian made as if to argue and then shrugged helplessly at Barbara.

Susan clung to Barbara, her Joan of Arc features filled with desperation. 'Barbara, *must* you leave us?' she implored.

Unseen by the others, the Doctor's face betrayed the hope that Ian and Barbara would change their minds, and he listened intently to the ensuing conversation while pretending to examine a faulty circuit panel.

Barbara smiled sadly. 'Susan, Ian and I have had some terrific adventures with you and your grandfather, but you always knew that we intended to return home to Earth in the end, didn't you?' she said quietly.

Susan bit her lip miserably. 'Yes, I know, but . . . but it just won't be the same without you.'

Barbara put her hands on the girl's shoulders. 'I know it's hard to say goodbye, Susan, especially after everything we've been through together,' she said gently, 'but one day you'll understand why Ian and I must leave you now.'

'But Barbara, the TARDIS can bring you back to Earth at any time.'

Ian came over and put his arm affectionately round Susan's waist. 'The longer we stay together the harder it will become to say goodbye,' he explained kindly.

Susan stared at each of them in turn. 'Oh well, if you both insist on going back to your dreary old routine at Coal Hill School . . . ' she retorted petulantly.

Shaking his head despondently, the Doctor deftly removed a small circuit panel from underneath the console and studied it closely, still eavesdropping intently.

Susan impulsively kissed Barbara and Ian and then ran out of the control chamber through one of the internal doors, leaving the two schoolteachers face to face and utterly disheartened.

After a few moments the Doctor turned round suddenly and bumped into them. 'Oh, still here, are we?' he snapped irritably, peering at the circuits.

Ian Chesterton smiled sourly. 'Yes, Doctor, we're still waiting for you to carry out the routine checks.'

The old man waved the circuit panel dismissively in Ian's face. 'That will be quite unnecessary, Chesterton.'

Ian glanced wryly at Barbara. 'Will it, Doctor? Are you

quite certain you know where we are?'

'And *when* we are?' Barbara added pointedly.

The Time Lord's mouth turned down even more as he squinted imperiously along his nose at the sceptical humans. His high, domed forehead wrinkled in a contemptuous frown. 'Certain? Of course I'm certain!' he rapped indignantly.

The other two stared doubtfully at the quietly humming control console and then back at the Doctor.

'Very well, see for yourselves . . . ' he cried testily, leaning over and flicking a switch.

A monitor screen suspended above the console flashed into life. When the static had cleared, they saw the dark outline of huge trees silhouetted against the evening sky.

'There. Are you satisfied now?'

Barbara Wright gazed at the eerie scene on the monitor and her face relaxed into its customary expression of mild superiority. 'Well, I suppose it *could* be Earth,' she granted reluctantly.

The Doctor sighed with exasperation. 'Then I'll give you a telephoto view . . . ' he muttered, adjusting the controls so that the monitor zoomed through the foliage to reveal vast fields under a huge lowering sky.

'It's a pity it's so dark,' Ian commented, screwing up his eyes at the scene above their heads. 'There's no sign of any buildings or anything.'

Barbara suddenly looked a little happier. 'It reminds me of a holiday I once spent in Somerset.'

The Doctor switched off the scanner. 'Then I expect that it *is* Somerset, young woman.' He touched another switch and a door-shaped portion of the chamber wall swung smoothly open with a quiet hiss. He held out his hand and then abruptly changed the gesture into a cursory wave. 'If you two are going then you might as well go,' he said curtly, frowning at the small circuit panel he was still holding.

After a moment's hesitation Ian strode over to the Doctor. 'I think it might be advisable if you came with us,' he suggested with a knowing look.

The Time Lord glanced up sharply. 'I shall do no such thing! I refuse to leave the TARDIS.'

Ian smiled indulgently. 'Doctor, you've taken us "home" once before,' he said sarcastically.

Barbara joined them. 'Yes, and we bumped straight into Marco Polo!' she added.

'So what makes you think you've succeeded this time?' Ian demanded.

The Doctor banged the circuitry down on the console in exasperation. 'Young man, I've had quite enough of your impertinent insinuations that I am not in complete control of the TARDIS,' he declared acidly. 'I admit that it has developed the odd minor fault once or twice in the past. However . . . '

Ian realised that he would have to change his tactics if he was going to get anywhere. He put his arm round the Doctor's narrow shoulders. 'Of course you're in complete control, Doctor,' he said flatteringly. 'We know that you could revisit Earth any time you like.'

The Doctor nodded, somewhat pacified. 'Of course, quite a straightforward matter,' he agreed.

'But you may not find the time,' Ian went on smoothly. 'After all, your important research must be completed, mustn't it? So it's quite possible we shall never meet again.'

At first Barbara had been taken aback by Ian's peculiar behaviour, but she quickly saw what he was up to. With a winning smile she straightened the Doctor's cravat, brushed the dust off his lapels and nodded her agreement.

'So don't you think we should part under more friendly circumstances?' Ian suggested. 'Say over a drink or something?'

The Doctor stood flanked by the two smiling teachers, glancing hesitantly from one to the other and pursing his thin lips thoughtfully as he considered Ian's proposal. 'Why not?' he eventually responded. 'Yes, perhaps Susan and I will come with you. After all, an hour or two here and there won't come amiss, will it?'

Barbara glanced ruefully at Ian. 'Here and there . . . ?' she whispered behind the Doctor's back, recalling the Time Lord's previous attempts to return them to their proper place and time in his Time And Relative Dimensions in Space machine.

The Doctor grinned at them. 'Susan? Susan, bring me my stick!' he called with sudden cheerful enthusiasm.

Susan came running into the chamber through the internal door, hastily wiping her eyes with a handkerchief. 'Yes, Grandfather?' she cried hopefully.

'Fetch my stick, child,' the Doctor ordered briskly. 'I have decided that we should see Ian and Barbara safely home before we depart from the galaxy.'

Susan clapped her hands in delight and hurried to bring the Doctor's silver-knobbed walking stick.

Barbara touched Ian's arm. 'Good work, she murured apprehensively. 'But are we really home at last?'

Ian gave a hollow laugh and shrugged. 'We'll soon find out,' he muttered stoically.

The Doctor locked the door of the TARDIS, pocketed the key and strode across the gloomy forest clearing swinging his stick and gazing keenly around as he sniffed the hot muggy air with a critical frown. With his body temperature of just sixty degrees Fahrenheit, the Time Lord knew that he was going to find Earth uncomfortably warm as usual. Still, he could not help having a soft spot for these infuriating humans, and he was as curious as they were to discover exactly where the police box had landed them this time.

Susan, Barbara and Ian were gazing through a gap in the trees at the rolling fields beyond the edge of the dark forest.

'It's very warm, it must be summertime,' Susan said eagerly. 'But why can't we see any lights or anything?'

'Towns and villages can be quite far apart, even in England,' Barbara pointed out, as if giving a geography lesson.

The Doctor joined them. 'Are we going to stand here gossiping all night?' he demanded, peering at the silent landscape.

Next moment two noises like gunshots rang out in the distance and the undergrowth behind the TARDIS stirred and rustled.

Susan jumped and nudged Ian.

'All right. I saw it . . . ' Ian whispered out of the corner of his mouth. 'Keep talking, Susan.' Ian moved away towards the mysterious thicket, his body tensed for action.

'Did you see what it was?' Barbara murmured into Susan's ear.

Before Susan could respond, the Doctor turned to them sharply. 'I'm not deaf, Miss Wright!' he snapped. 'It's probably a rabbit or something,' he added nonchalantly, staring after Ian. 'You know, young Chesterton's getting quite jumpy. Young chaps like him shouldn't suffer from nerves.'

There was a shrill scream and a furious scuffling in the bushes behind the police box.

'That rabbit of yours is putting up quite a fight!' Barbara remarked caustically.

Next moment Ian appeared dragging a struggling urchin of about twelve by the collar of his ragged blouson shirt. The boy was fair-haired and freckled, his blue eyes wide with panic at the sight of the fierce old man and his companions. He was barefoot, with patched breeches flapping around his bony knees.

'Ian, you're hurting him!' Barbara protested.

'No, I'm not . . . ' Ian retorted, blowing on his bitten fingers and glaring at his kicking and twisting captive.

'Come here, boy!' commanded the Doctor. 'Tell us where we are. Where do you live?'

'Grandfather, you're frightening him,' Susan cried, running forward and putting her arm round the boy. 'We're friends. You needn't be afraid,' she told him gently.

The boy stopped struggling and stared uncomprehendingly, his eyes still wild with fear.

'He's terrified of us,' Barbara murmured, approaching slowly.

'Of us – or of something else?' Ian wondered, glancing round warily. 'If those were shots we heard just now . . . '

'Answer my questions, boy!' the Doctor ordered, striding over to him.

As the stern old man flourished his silver-headed cane at him the boy cowered. Then he muttered something in a hushed voice.

'He's speaking French!' Susan exclaimed in surprise.

Ian thought quickly. 'We will not hurt you . . . ' he told the boy in passable French.

'No, of course we will not. We need your help,' Barbara explained in much better French. 'We have lost our way.'

The boy drew closer to Susan as Ian relaxed his grip on him, but still kept silent.

Barbara tried again. 'Is this England?'

The boy frowned and shook his tousled head vigorously. 'England? No, this is France,' he declared proudly.

The strangers all glanced at one another in astonishment.

'France? How far are we from Paris?' Ian asked carefully.

The urchin pointed across the fields. 'Not far. Twelve kilometres perhaps.'

The Doctor smiled smugly. 'Paris, eh?' he muttered in English. 'Well a few hundred miles either way is only to be expected. After all, it is a minute fraction of the distance we have just travelled in the TARDIS.' He beamed approvingly across the clearing at the dilapidated police box. 'Quite accurate, in fact.'

'Not bad at all,' Ian agreed grudgingly. 'As long as distance is the only error.'

'Just what do you mean by that, young man?' the Doctor shouted, his eyes blazing with resentment.

'A few hundred *years* either way . . . ?' Ian mocked, nudging Barbara.

'Nonsense!' spluttered the Doctor. '*I'll* have a word with the lad.'

The Doctor started to ask the boy a question in immaculate French. Finding himself momentarily unguarded, the urchin took advantage of the strangers' confusion. Wriggling out of Susan's grasp, he took to his heels and vanished into the tangled undergrowth like a rabbit.

'Grab him, Chesterton!' the Doctor shouted, lashing out vainly with his walking stick. But it was too late. The lad had disappeared into the twilight.

'We'll never catch him now,' Ian mumbled shame-facedly.

'I wonder what he was so afraid of?' Susan murmured, glancing apprehensively around the clearing.

15

'Did you notice his clothes?' Barbara said thoughtfully. 'They were very old-fashioned.'

Ian nodded grimly and turned to the Doctor. 'So, we know *where* we are, Doctor. But do we know *when*?'

Not far away, in a hollow in the middle of the fields, stood a derelict farmhouse half-hidden in a small copse of tall poplars. The crumbling stone building formed an 'L' shape enclosing a paved yard with a similarly shaped group of adjoining barns and outbuildings. In the shadow of the nearby trees, the grimy cobweb-festooned windows stared out like sightless eyes. The yard itself was strewn with rotting straw, broken tiles and glass, and tall weeds sprang up everywhere between the uneven cobbles. Rusting and decaying items of farm machinery were heaped in corners. In the centre of the yard was a deep dark well, its broken winch roofed with ravaged thatch. The well looked like the entrance to some goblin's subterranean kingdom in a fairy tale.

Suddenly the humid silence was shattered by the shrill squeak of rusted hinges and the huge farmyard gate swung open and banged against the archway between the barns and the stables. The young boy from the forest ran across the yard and over to the porch and peered through the filthy panes in the worm-eaten front door. Inside, a faint yellow candle was burning in the murky darkness. Glancing furtively over his shoulder, as if fearful of being followed, the boy banged on the door in a series of staccato beats, like a sort of code. A few seconds later the door opened with an eerie groan. The boy gave a final look round and then darted inside, slamming the door behind him.

A little later the candle was blown out and the house waited, lifeless and dark among the forbidding trees.

The four travellers stood at the edge of the fields, peering through the gloom at the blank windows of the farmhouse among the clustering trees.

'Human habitation at last,' the Doctor announced, pointing with his walking stick.

'What do you make of it, Barbara,' asked Ian without

enthusiasm. The farm hardly looked very welcoming after their epic journeys in the TARDIS.

'Looks deserted,' Barbara replied. 'You know, I'm convinced we've landed some time in the past.'

The Doctor grunted non-commitally but said nothing.

Ian looked distinctly uneasy as he glanced up at the darkening sky. 'I'm beginning to feel we should get back to the TARDIS while we can,' he confessed.

'Nonsense!' snapped the Doctor. 'It was your idea to explore, Chesterton. It could be rather interesting. Besides, the walk will do us all good.' Swinging his stick like an eager hiker, the Time Lord set off across the field at a cracking pace, whistling merrily and recklessly slashing at the long seedy grass stalks.

Susan followed her grandfather after a momentary hesitation. 'Come on, you two,' she called over her shoulder. 'We don't want to lose each other in the dark, do we?'

'Don't worry, we're right behind you . . .' Ian answered reluctantly, as he and Barbara tailed along at a more leisurely pace.

Barbara stared disapprovingly at the Doctor's fast-receding back. 'We're still nowhere near home,' she complained bitterly.

Ian shrugged resignedly. 'At least the Doctor tried. We must be grateful for that, I suppose.'

'So we're staying with the TARDIS after all?'

Ian shrugged again and grinned. 'Well, it's cheered Susan up if nothing else,' he said amiably.

Barbara shot Ian a puzzled sidelong glance. 'You seem quite keen to stay all of a sudden''

Ian shrugged a third time. 'I could change my mind,' he laughed. 'It all depends on *when* we are!'

Suddenly they heard Susan's urgent calls from the trees around the farmhouse. 'Ian . . . Barbara . . . Come quickly!'

'Here we go again . . .' Ian muttered ruefully. 'Come on, Barbara.'

Susan peered over the Doctor's shoulder as he squinted through the cobweb-encrusted panes in the farmhouse

17

porch. 'They're just coming, Grandfather,' she whispered.

The Doctor wiped the filthy window with his sleeve. 'It seems to be utterly derelict,' he murmured. 'I wonder if we can get inside.'

The farmyard gate shrieked and made them jump.

'Have you found anything interesting?' Barbara asked breathlessly, running up to them.

Susan shook her head. 'Grandfather wants to get inside.'

'Does he now!' Ian exclaimed doubtfully, striding into the porch.

The Doctor pushed him towards the window. 'Chesterton, take a look. Your eyes should be sharper than mine.'

Stifling a protest, Ian pressed his face to the blank window. 'I don't think anyone's lived here for years,' he said, brushing the dirt from his cheek.

But the Doctor was already hopping mischievously inside. 'We're in luck!' he crowed. 'The front door's unlocked.'

The others followed warily as the Doctor ventured into a dark low-ceilinged room sparsely furnished with a few broken chairs, a rickety table and an old wooden trunk with brass corners. Everything was covered in a thick layer of dust and hardly any daylight penetrated the cracked and grimy panes. On the table, a pair of tarnished but ornate candlesticks looked oddly out of place in such humble surroundings. Susan gasped and drew back in horror as a huge feathery cobweb wafted against her cheek in the doorway.

The Doctor unearthed a small tinderbox from a drawer and after a few unsuccessful attempts, he finally managed to produce a good enough spark to light one of the stumps of candle. 'Good,' he cried triumphantly. 'I'll search upstairs. Chesterton, you take a look down here.'

Ian held back uneasily as the Doctor started to climb the narrow, dark stairs leading up from the corner of the room opposite the door. But as the old man's footsteps receded, he pulled himself together and set about lighting the second candle. It sputtered intermittently for a few seconds and then gave a steady, if smoky yellow flame.

'Where's the Doctor gone?' asked Barbara, edging nervously into the room behind Susan.

'Exploring upstairs.' Ian held out the tinderbox. 'What do

you make of this, Barbara?' he whispered, so that Susan, who had started rummaging in the old trunk in the corner, would not hear.

'It must be hundreds of years old,' Barbara murmured.

They both jumped as Susan emitted a loud sneeze from the dust getting up her nose. 'Look at these,' Susan exclaimed, holding up some old clothes she had found folded in the trunk.

Barbara picked up a very full-skirted dress in faded brocade material and held it against herself. 'It's all eighteenth century stuff!' she gasped in astonishment.

'Look at this one,' Susan said excitedly, unfolding a lowcut dress with frilly elbow-length sleeves, decorated bodice and billowing full-length skirt. It was almost exactly her size.

Barbara rummaged in the trunk and pulled out several more outfits, both women's and men's, from the same period. 'There's a complete wardrobe here . . . Different sizes too!'

Ian brought the candlestick over. 'Look at these little bundles.' He unearthed several oddly shaped packages and proceeded to undo them. They contained bottles of wine and lumps of stale grey bread.

Under the clothes, Barbara had discovered some ornate daggers, several rolled-up maps and a bundle of documents. Ian scanned the documents by the feeble flickering candle-light. 'These look like letters of authority,' he murmured. 'The names of the holders are still blank. I think they're passes of some kind,' he said, showing the papers to the girls.

Susan sneezed mightily again as she tried on the dress with the pretty bodice.

'Yet nobody seems to live here now,' Barbara pointed out. 'Just look at all the dust.'

'Perhaps the house is some kind of refuge,' Ian suggested vaguely. 'These could be supplies for some sort of escape route.'

'How romantic!' Barbara teased as he unrolled a fresh batch of documents. Then her face became deadly serious as she read the elaborate copperplate handwriting over Ian's shoulder. 'This one's signed by *Robespierre*!' she gasped,

19

clasping Ian's arm. 'And look at the date, Ian: *Deuxième Thermidor* . . . ' Barbara's mouth fell open and she gaped at Ian in disbelief. 'It must be the French Revolution!' she finally managed to say.

Ian stared back at her. 'You mean the Doctor's dropped us bang in the middle of the French Revolution?' he said incredulously.

Barbara took the document and examined the date again. 'The Second *Thermidor* . . . That's July, 1794 . . . ' she said in a strange hollow voice. 'If I'm right, the Doctor's dropped us bang in the middle of the Terror!'

2

Under Siege

The Doctor had crept cautiously up the narrow creaking staircase and along a cramped and dusty passage leading off the landing on the upper floor. His flickering candle flame showed several doors leading off on either side.

He tried the handles and discovered that one or two were locked, but most swung open with a squeak and a shower of choking dust to reveal an empty little room or a room piled with broken bits of furniture. It was obvious that the farm-house had been deserted for many years. Raising the candle-stick high, the Doctor peered into the cobwebby shadows and every few paces he stopped and listened. Once or twice he fancied he could detect the sound of heavy breathing, but soon he decided that his imagination was playing tricks. He was about to give up his search for something interesting and retrace his steps downstairs, when he suddenly heard a sinister creaking noise at the other end of the long passage. Grasping his stick firmly in one hand and the heavy candle-stick in the other, he advanced towards the source of the ominous noise, his eyes darting from side to side and his wiry body tensed, ready to defend himself against attack.

He had almost reached the end of the passage when something stirred in an open doorway beside him. Before he could react, a hand flew out of the darkness and a heavy pistol butt struck him a glancing blow on the back of the head. With a muffled gasp he sank to his knees and keeled over sideways, still clutching the stick and the candle. A boot emerged from the shadows and trod out the candle flame. Then there was silence once more.

In the room below, Susan had finished changing into the long dress and Barbara was struggling into a plainer lowcut dress which was just a little too small for her. Ian had donned a pair of black velvet breeches, whitish stockings and a white shirt with full sleeves and frilled front, and he was just cramming his feet into elegantly buckled black shoes.

'How do I look, Ian?' Barbara asked, sucking in her tummy and shaking out the skirts.

Ian grinned. 'Not bad, Barbara. The hairstyle's a bit nineteen-sixties though,' he replied, ruffling the side parting out of his own short hair and smoothing it back off his forehead.

They gathered round the candle on the table and scrutinised each other critically, like guests at a fancy dress party.

'It was a jolly good idea of yours to dress up in this gear, Susan,' Ian said approvingly. 'Now we won't look quite so conspicuous if any of the inhabitants do see us.'

Susan giggled. 'We'd better not let Grandfather know that we've arrived during the Reign of Terror,' she said mischievously.

'Why not?' Ian asked.

'Because it's his favourite period in terrestrial history. We'll never get away.'

Barbara suddenly remembered something that had happened the day she and Ian had first met the Doctor and been abducted in the TARDIS. 'Is that why you wanted to borrow the book about the French Revolution, Susan?'

Before their former pupil could answer, Ian strode across to the doorway leading to the staircase in the corner. 'Doctor? Where are you? What on earth are you doing up there?' he demanded. His voice echoed eerily around the farmhouse and died away.

They listened to the silence. Susan and Barbara began to look anxious.

Ian snatched up the candle. 'Let's go and find the old fool,' he suggested, a note of concern creeping into his irritation.

22

Susan and Barbara followed him towards the stairs. But before Ian could put his foot on the first step, he found himself staring into the barrel of a cocked flintlock pistol. The girls recoiled in shock, but before they could turn and flee a second pistol whipped out of the gloom and covered them. Two young Frenchmen emerged from the shadows of the doorway and stared at them with cold hostile eyes. Ian and the girls backed away. Suddenly Ian drew back his arm to hurl the candlestick in the strangers' faces.

'Do not move!' rapped one of them. He gestured at the candlestick with his pistol. 'Please put that on the table slowly.'

Ian hesitated for a moment, laboriously translating the order in his head. Then he sullenly obeyed.

The Frenchmen advanced warily into the room. The one who had spoken was about thirty years old. He had dark shoulder-length hair and a large mouth. He seemed calm and appeared to be in charge. His companion was younger and fair-haired. He seemed edgy and frightened and could not keep still. Both men wore plainish cutaway tailcoats with high collars and large lapels. Their shirts had frilled cuffs and plain cravats and their breeches were tucked into tall boots.

'Do not waste time, Rouvray,' muttered the younger man nervously. 'Kill them. They would have killed us.'

Rouvray held up his hand for silence. 'What are you people doing here?' he demanded icily, his eyes boring like gimlets into Ian's in the candlelight.

'It is obvious. They are after us!' the younger man shouted.

'No, d'Argenson, I think not,' Rouvray snapped. 'Answer my question!' he ordered, aiming his pistol at Ian's head.

The three travellers stared at their captors in speechless panic. Eventually Ian opened his mouth, but no sounds came out.

'We are travellers . . . We stopped here to ask the way . . . ' Barbara and Susan suddenly burst out in unison in very good French.

Rouvray smiled sardonically. 'At a deserted house?'

D'Argenson waved his pistol impatiently in their faces.

'We shall gain nothing by this questioning. We must be on our way,' he insisted. 'Kill them and have done with it.'

Rouvray shook his head. 'Patience, d'Argenson. Even in these terrible times people should have the right to justify themselves . . . even though our enemies do not accord us such privileges.'

Ian took a deep breath. 'We are not your enemies,' he said in halting French. 'We are merely travellers. That is all you need to know.'

Rouvray stepped closer, still aiming his pistol unerringly between Ian's eyes. 'When you entered our refuge you entered our lives,' he declared mysteriously. 'Do you travel alone?'

There was a tense pause.

'Yes, we do,' Barbara said eventually.

'D'Argenson's eyes lit up in cruel triumph. 'You see? They lie!' he shouted.

Once again the elder stranger gestured to his friend to keep calm. 'We found an old man upstairs,' he revealed, glancing from Ian to the two girls and back again. 'Do not count on his assistance.'

Susan tried to spring forward, but Barbara held her back. 'What have you done to him?' she demanded, suddenly unafraid.

Rouvray gazed accusingly at the defiant teenager. 'It was in your power to see that he came to no harm,' he retorted. 'At the moment he is safe.' His eyes narrowed. 'Your answer proved that you do not speak truthfully. You are concealing something.'

'I told you before, it does not concern you,' Ian persisted firmly but politely.

D'Argenson had started pacing agitatedly around the gloomy room. 'We must go at once, Rouvray,' he urged. 'The soldiers could have followed us here.'

Rouvray stared hard at Ian. 'In France now there are two sides only and you are either with us or against us.' He paused. 'Our sympathies are obvious. We have to know yours.'

Barbara stepped forward cautiously. 'We appreciate what you say, but I assure you that we have no loyalty to either side. We are not even French . . . ' she explained as reasonably as she could.

D'Argenson banged his pistol on the table. 'They are foreign agents. It is obvious!' he spat contemptuously.

Rouvray considered Barbara's words for a moment, studying the three captives in turn. Then he slowly lowered his pistol and uncocked it. 'A word of warning my friends,' he said solemnly, putting the pistol away in his belt. 'If you intend to remain in France you will have to choose: one side or the other.'

D'Argenson was still brandishing his pistol at the captives. 'We cannot possibly trust these people now!' he protested, feverishly seizing his associate's arm, his eyes blazing with fanatical zeal.

Calmly Rouvray eased the pistol out of d'Argenson's hand, uncocked it and put it in d'Argenson's coat. 'If we are to escape from France we must have faith,' he argued earnestly. 'If we can trust no-one then we shall simply be taking the Terror with us wherever we go.'

'But we must find Grandfather,' Susan exclaimed, as if they had forgotten all about the Doctor. 'Where is he?'

Rouvray turned to d'Argenson. 'The old man . . . ?'

'Listen!' Ian had been trying to identify a faint noise outside. He flung up his hand and everyone held their breath.

In the distance they could just make out the sound of a party of men shouting and laughing as they approached the farmhouse.

Ian moved to the window just as the farmyard gate swung open with its habitual shriek of rusted hinges. Peering through the filthy panes, he made out the figures of a couple of officers and a bunch of soldiers entering the yard. 'Soldiers . . . ' he muttered.

D'Argenson grabbed Rouvray's sleeve. 'They've found us . . . What did I tell you?' he groaned in despair. 'Now will you believe me!'

'Quiet!' Rouvray snapped, moving swiftly to extinguish the candle and then joining Ian at the window.

Armed with swords and muskets with gleaming bayonets fixed to the barrels, the soldiers were now advancing on the house. Their uniforms were ragged and dusty, with a motley mixture of styles. Most wore tall, crescent-shaped black hats with tricolour cockades, blue coats with gold epaulettes and crossed white straps, and buff breeches tucked into boots. Some brandished flaming torches as well as weapons. They looked dangerously undisciplined and their sergeant was obviously drunk.

Hearing the menacing clump of their boots on the cobblestones, d'Argenson backed away from the window clutching his head distraughtly. 'They will take us to Paris, to the guillotine . . . ' he gasped. 'Rouvray, you know I cannot let it happen . . . I cannot . . . ' The terrified young man grabbed Susan's and Barbara's arms and began to pour out his tragic personal story. 'My whole family was executed even my younger sister . . . ' he stuttered. 'The soldiers burst into the house . . . I was absent . . . And they dragged them all away to the *Place de la Révolution* where the guillotine . . . '

'*Place de Louis Quinze* . . . ' Rouvray corrected him, as though by insisting on the original names he could somehow turn back the clock and unmake the cataclysmic events of the previous five years.

This was too much for d'Argenson. His voice disintegrated into sobs and he flung himself frantically on Rouvray. 'We must flee while we have the chance!' he screamed.

Rouvray seized his hands and endeavoured to calm him. 'They would see us. Our only hope now is to hide here,' he said firmly.

Ian swung round, his face pale in the darkness. 'They are coming in,' he muttered grimly.

In futile desperation d'Argenson tried to drag Rouvray towards the door. 'It will be the guillotine for us . . . ' he screamed hysterically.

Rouvray struck his friend sharply across the face with the palm of his hand. D'Argenson stared at him in astonishment and then sank to his knees in despair. Rouvray removed the pistol from d'Argenson's coat and handed it to Ian. The Englishman took the weapon, tentatively smiling his thanks and then turned back to the window.

Behind the table, Barbara held Susan close to her side and put her finger to her lips. The bright torchlight lit up their frightened faces as they watched the window and waited, barely breathing.

Outside, the sergeant who was a bloated brutal peasant with a red face and small malevolent eyes, had ordered his men to halt. A few moments later a young lieutenant marched into the farmyard followed by another motley rabble, some half in uniform and carrying an odd assortment of weapons. The lieutenant wore a long cloak over his tunic and a large tricolour plume in his hat.

The sergeant stabbed a stubby finger at the windows of the farmhouse. 'The pigs will still be running, Citizen. They won't have stopped yet,' he growled, spitting in the straw.

The officer shook his head. 'According to our intelligence this is their first refuge from Paris, Sergeant. They could well be hiding here, waiting to proceed under cover of darkness,' he declared with chilling menace.

The sergeant shrugged and belched. 'I'll send the lads in to search . . . '

The lieutenant raised his hand. 'No! Let the men rest. They have had a tiring march.' He smiled maliciously. 'We shall simply surround the house. If our friends are in there they can enjoy the suspense while we wait.'

The sergeant gestured at a bunch of slouching soldiers. 'We'll block their escape!' he roared. 'Go round the back, boys.'

'Go yourself, Citizen!' one of them retorted.

The motley troop chuckled and nudged each other.

The sergeant winked at the impudent private. 'But if the rabbits run, you'll get a chance to catch them, won't you?' he growled contemptuously.

The soldier thought for a moment and then grinned broadly. 'Yes, it's a long time since I had a royalist to myself,' he sneered with grimacing *double-entendre*.

His lounging fellows chuckled raucously.

'Keep your eyes open then,' the sergeant ordered encouragingly.

'Don't you worry, they won't get past *me*,' the soldier promised, moving off towards the gate.

'Nor me . . . Nor me . . . ' chorused several other peasant

militiamen, snatching up their weapons and following him eagerly.

The remaining troops sat around on the broken farm carts and ploughs, chatting and playing cards. The lieutenant sat on the edge of the well and watched the house, while the sergeant shuffled impatiently up and down, belching and spitting and scratching himself.

Inside the dark farmhouse it was deathly still as the five besieged refugees waited for the attack. Ian and Rouvray flanked the window, pistols cocked at the ready. Barbara and Susan huddled behind the table and kept their eyes on the door. D'Argenson sat slumped by the table close to breaking point. Sweating and wide-eyed with fear, he gnawed at his knuckles, stifling the urge to argue with Rouvray and struggling to decide whether to make a break for it on his own.

At the window, Rouvray had been giving a hurriedly whispered account of the events leading up to their present desperate predicament. Ian and the girls had managed to understand most of the story so far.

' . . . and then we were warned to leave France at once or risk arrest and execution. Friends warn us. Friends denounce us . . . ' he concluded with a sigh.

'The soldiers followed you here. Who would have known you were taking this route?' Ian asked him quietly.

Rouvray shrugged. 'Who indeed? It is difficult to have secrets these days.'

Ian peered cautiously through the window. 'They are not coming in . . . ' he murmured, surprised and puzzled.

Rouvray turned to look at d'Argenson's trembling figure. 'No. They intend to break our nerve,' he said bitterly.

Susan plucked up courage to speak. 'What did you do with my grandfather?' she asked out of the shadows.

Rouvray gestured at his friend. 'D'Argenson dealt with him. He is somewhere upstairs . . . ' he said vaguely.

Ian uttered a muffled exclamation of guilt at having neglected the Doctor so long. 'I'll go and find him, Susan,' he said in English.

'Be careful, Ian,' Barbara murmured as he edged away

from the window and disappeared through the doorway and up the stairs.

All at once d'Argenson jumped to his feet and hurled himself at the door leading outside.

Rouvray tried to grab him as he passed. 'Come back, you fool, come back!' he muttered through clenched teeth.

But he was too late. D'Argenson had fled outside.

The lounging soldiers got slowly to their feet, staring almost hungrily at the dishevelled and wild-eyed figure emerging from the porch into the courtyard. They raised their fire-brands and picked up their muskets in anticipation of a kill. After a few faltering steps towards the gate, d'Argenson stopped in his tracks and watched like a mesmerised animal as the sergeant and his ragged troops slowly closed in on him. The lieutenant, who had remained seated on the wall of the well watching with cynical amusement, suddenly stood up as he saw Rouvray coming out of the house behind them.

'Sergeant . . . There's Rouvray!' he shouted.

The sergeant turned and some of the troops started converging on the tall, almost noble figure standing in the porch.

'Do not move!' Rouvray suddenly commanded, his rich voice ringing impressively round the yard. 'Get away from d'Argenson.'

'Take that traitor Rouvray!' the lieutenant ordered, the plumes in his hat quivering with the force of his indignation.

'No. You will listen to me!' Rouvray countermanded imperiously, holding his ground. The butt of his pistol could just be seen protruding from his pocket, but he looked quite defenceless.

The rabble of soldiers hesitated in an embarrassed huddle, unsure what to do next. The sergeant's blotchy face was livid, but he kept quiet and waited to see what the citizens would decide.

The lieutenant smiled sourly. 'So, Rouvray, your voice still carries authority, even among my soldiers,' he conceded jealously.

Rouvray surveyed the sullen, fidgeting militiamen with a contemptuous glare. 'You . . . Come here!' he rapped,

29

pointing to a youth wearing a tattered military coat over his
sans-culotte trousers who was holding his musket like a pickaxe.

The lad shuffled obediently forward.

'Give me your weapon,' Rouvray ordered.

Like an automaton the confused youth handed over his
musket with mute submissiveness.

Rouvray took it and flung it scornfully at the lieutenant's
feet. 'There, Lieutenant. You can give them uniforms and
weapons but they remain peasants underneath . . . ' he
scoffed.

Unnoticed by anyone else, the sergeant had levelled his
musket at Rouvray. Just as the fugitive royalist opened his
mouth to continue his harangue, the sergeant fired. Rouvray
stood quite still for a moment, his jaw hanging open and an
astonished look on his handsome face. Then he fell forward
flat on his face in the straw, dead.

With a hoarse shriek, d'Argenson took to his heels across
the yard, desperately making for the open gate under the
archway.

'Stick the pig!' yelled the sergeant, urging his men in
pursuit.

Their bayonets flashing in the torchlight, the mob easily
cornered the hapless d'Argenson by the gateway. The lieutenant watched grim-faced as the bristling bayonets rose
and fell over the screaming victim. Then he turned abruptly
and strode over to Rouvray's motionless body. 'A desperate
attempt . . . ' he murmured almost sympathetically, stirring
the corpse with his boot. 'And it very nearly worked.'

A hearty cheer burst from the execution squad as they
wiped d'Argenson's blood from their gleaming blades.

The lieutenant looked up and grimaced with distaste.
'The People must have their revenge . . . ' he sighed,
shaking his head.

With the unfamiliar pistol held out in front of him as though
it were liable to go off by itself, Ian Chesterton was edging
his way cautiously along the upstairs passage. Without a
candle he could see virtually nothing in the darkness and he
was forced to rely on touch. He tried the doors as he passed

30

and groped blindly about in those rooms he did manage to get into. 'Doctor? Doctor, where are you . . . ?' he called, expecting any moment to stumble over a fallen body. He stopped and listened for the sound of groans or muffled cries, but there was nothing, no trace of the Doctor anywhere.

He was about to go on, when suddenly a piercing scream came from downstairs. It sounded like Susan. Then Ian heard Barbara's panic-stricken voice pleading 'No . . . No . . . No . . . ' Ian turned and felt his way back to the staircase as fast as he could. He crashed down the narrow stairs and stumbled into the torch-lit room.

As he came through the door, a musket sliced out of the shadows and smashed the pistol out of his hand. Then he was seized from behind and forced over to the table. Behind it cowered Susan and Barbara guarded by two soldiers. The lieutenant was standing in the doorway from the porch with his hands on his hips, grinning with satisfaction.

'My sergeant was quite right,' he declared smugly. 'It *did* pay us to look in the house, after all.'

Ian struggled to free himself from the two militiamen who were holding his arms behind his back. 'But we . . . we have no connection with . . . ' he began, searching his memory for the words in French.

The lieutenant strode forward and thrust his face into Ian's. '*Silence*!' he hissed. Then he marched slowly round and round the table as if uncertain what he should do next. 'If any of them speak again without permission, shoot them,' he ordered.

The soldiers nodded eagerly and levelled their muskets at their three silent captives. Ian heard Susan gasp with fright, but he could only exchange helpless glances with Barbara.

A few minutes later, the sergeant stomped into the room and his puffy features lit up when he saw the prisoners, especially the two girls. 'The bodies have been disposed of, Citizen,' he reported gruffly. 'What about this lot?'

The officer made up his mind. 'Outside,' he snapped, jerking his head at the door.

The sergeant prodded Ian with his musket butt. 'You heard the citizen, come on outside . . . '

31

While the soldiers shoved their captives into the yard, the officer lingered in the room for a few minutes studying the maps and documents from the trunk. He examined the fake passes with particular satisfaction. Finally he rolled the papers up and put them in his pocket and marched out into the yard with a cruel smile playing on his callow features.

Ian, Susan and Barbara had been roughly tied up to a dilapidated old haycart and the sergeant had drawn his men up in front of them in two ranks, like a firing squad. Grinning at his victims with brutal glee, the sergeant raised his sword high in the air.

'Prime muskets . . . ' he ordered.

'We already have,' yelled one of the soldiers. 'Get out of the way.'

'Take aim . . . ' croaked the sergeant, swaggering tipsily out of the line of fire as the dozen or so muskets were levelled at the trembling, white-faced prisoners.

Speechless with horror, Barbara and Susan watched the sword as it waved about uncertainly above the sergeant's head, ready to signal the squad to fire. Ian struggled frantically to free his hands and feet from the crude bonds, but there was little he could do even if he did manage to break away.

Gleaming in the torchlight, the sergeant's sword twitched spasmodically. Next moment it would slash through the air signalling the end for the helpless prisoners.

'Stop!'

The lieutenant strode out of the house, his eyes blazing with anger. 'We take them to Paris,' he bellowed, marching between the muskets and the three ashen-faced victims.

The soldiers groaned with disappointment.

'I say we shoot them now,' argued the sergeant, still brandishing his sword.

'Listen to me,' said the lieutenant calmly. 'We have captured suspected foreign agents. Do you not want to take the credit, my friends?'

There was a rumble of discussion among the troops.

'Just imagine how eager Citizen Lemaître will be to interrogate them,' the officer added cunningly.

32

At the mention of Lemaître everyone fell silent.

'That's true . . . ' growled the sergeant, sheathing his sword. 'And there might be a reward!'

Susan, Barbara and Ian hung in their bonds bathed in sweat and shaking with fear as their fate was debated in front of them.

The officer nodded vigorously. 'The citizen sergeant is quite right. Perhaps there will be a reward,' he agreed persuasively. 'And why should we try to do what Madame Guillotine can do much more elegantly?'

The troops laughed and nudged each other and nodded their assent.

'We'll take them to Paris!' shouted the sergeant contentedly.

'To Paris! To the guillotine!' the troops chorused enthusiastically, shouldering their weapons. One or two of them hastened over to cut the prisoners loose. Then they drove them out of the farmyard like cattle, with the lieutenant following at a haughty distance behind the ragged procession.

The sergeant lingered in the yard with several of the militiamen who were carrying flaring torches. He grabbed one of the firebrands and flung it into the hayloft next to the house. With a savage cheer, the others threw their torches into the tinder dry barns and outhouses and up at the farmhouse windows. Within seconds the straw and wood caught fiercely alight and the fire spread greedily, crackling and roaring along the timbers and out of the windows in long hot tongues. Showers of sparks exploded into the darkness, provoking cheers from the happy arsonists. Reluctantly the sergeant led his men to catch up with the others on the track leading to the Paris road.

'The house . . . Look at the house . . . ' Barbara gasped, turning as she heard the crackle of glass and the clatter of dislodged slates from the roof.

Susan clung tearfully to Ian's arm. 'Wasn't there any sign of Grandfather at all?' she beseeched him.

The soldiers herded them onwards with their bayonets and musket butts.

'He must have got out some other way,' Barbara

murmured comfortingly as they stumbled on again, but her despairing glance to Ian betrayed her worst fears.

'I hope so . . . ' Ian muttered, putting his arm round Susan and helping her along. 'I hope so for all our sakes . . . '

With a vicious oath, the sergeant came up and shoved them forward along the stony track skirting the edge of the bleak dark forest, as if he could not wait to get them to Paris.

Unseen by anyone, a small figure was crouching in the undergrowth beside the track and when the straggling column had passed safely by, the foliage parted and the pale freckled face of the little peasant boy emerged and watched until the soldiers were swallowed up in the darkness. Then the boy sprang out of the bushes and started running towards the blazing farmhouse among the trees.

The Doctor had come to with a splitting headache and a very stiff neck and his throat was parched from the dust in the tiny boxroom in which d'Argenson had locked him. He found himself lying on the floor with his head awkwardly bent up at an angle against the wall. He lay still, groaning and blinking his eyes to try and clear his blurred vision. Scarcely any light came through the small high window above him and he had no idea where he was. After a while he attempted to lever himself into a sitting position against the wall, but the effort was too great and he sank back on the dirty floorboards, half-conscious in the eerie silence.

Eventually he was roused by a strange banging and cracking noise. Suddenly he was seized by a fit of coughing and choking which brought him round and he realised that the boxroom was rapidly filling with smoke which was streaming in around the door and up between the rotting floorboards. Fighting the pain in his head and his neck, the Doctor rolled himself over onto his knees and forced himself up onto his feet. Snatching a handkerchief from his frock-coat he pressed it over his nose and his mouth, and groped his way around the walls until he reached the door. Choking and wheezing from the hot acrid smoke, he struggled with the handle and then began hammering for all he was worth and croaking as loudly as he could. 'Help me . . . Let me out . . . Let me out of here . . . '

But the relentless smoke seared his lungs and stung his watering eyes. He could feel the tremendous heat from the raging inferno all around him and the noise of the flames and the collapsing roof was deafening. Gradually he sank to the floor, desperately fighting to draw a little breath through the handkerchief and still hammering with one feeble fist on the walls and the floor in the vain hope that somehow somebody, somewhere, would find him and drag him to safety. But in no time at all the toxic smoke overwhelmed him. His fist knocked feebly on the floor for a few more seconds and then lay still . . .

3

Prisoners Of The People

The three prisoners and their ill-disciplined escort arrived at the *Conciergerie* in Paris at first light next morning. The atmosphere in the French capital was even more oppressive than it had been in the countryside. The weather was stiflingly hot and close and there was an air of menace and suspicion everywhere, as if nobody dared trust anybody else. People hurried about the narrow back streets with lowered eyes as though afraid to meet the gaze of others for fear of provoking some unfounded accusation concerning their loyalty to the Revolution. Soldiers of the citizens' militia – the *Garde Nationale* – were everywhere, and so were small bands of *sans-culottes* armed with muskets and dressed in their long trousers, baggy shirts and tall floppy hats turned over at the top like nightcaps with tricolour rosettes. The *sans-culottes* women also wore swords nonchalantly stuck in their belts as they clattered noisily across the cobbles in their wooden clogs.

Footsore and sweating from their exhausting trek, Susan, Barbara and Ian looked forward to the chance to rest, even though it was within the walls of the dreaded *Conciergerie* where prisoners for immediate execution or for quick token trial were taken for their short sojourn before death. At the gates, several toothless old women cackled heartily and waved their knitting needles with taunting spite as the victims were marched past into the courtyard.

'The famous *tricoteuses* . . . ' Barbara muttered with a shiver. 'Later on today they'll be sitting around the guillotine dipping their wool in the blood.' She couldn't resist a macabre smile to herself at the thought of an English

36

schoolteacher taking pupils on a tour of real historical events.

Susan clung to her arm and turned aside with a shudder as the soldiers shoved them roughly through the gates.

The prisoners were taken to a small room on one side of the courtyard where a fat judge dressed in a black robe and a white tabbed collar was sitting in an ornate chair at a small table covered in papers. The grey wig perched askew above his porridgy face looked filthy. Across his chest he wore a huge tricolour sash covered in foodstains. Several soldiers stood guard behind the captives and the lieutenant handed some documents to the wheezing and perspiring judge. There was a long pause while the judge perused the papers, occasionally writing with a scratchy quill.

'Are we to be allowed to tell our story?' Barbara eventually asked in respectful French.

The judge glared at her over his cracked pince-nez glasses. 'The accused are not required to speak,' he snapped, flourishing the papers. 'I have the charges and the evidence here.' He scanned the papers again and fixed the prisoners with cold, short-sighted eyes. 'You were found in the hide-out with Rouvray and d'Argenson . . . royalist counter-revolutionaries.'

Ian opened his mouth to speak, but the judge's baleful stare silenced him.

'I am satisfied as to your guilt,' the judge announced harshly. 'You are all sentenced to immediate execution.'

The fateful words rang in the bare stone room as the judge signed the execution order. The three companions stared aghast at one another. Ian thought for a moment of making a desperate attempt to escape.

'We demand the right to speak,' Barbara declared defiantly.

'You have no rights!' the judge shouted disdainfully. 'You will be guillotined as soon as it can be arranged.' He gestured to the guard with his quill. 'Take them to the cells immediately.'

As the time-travellers were manhandled across to the cells in the basement of the *Conciergerie*, they passed a huddle of dishevelled but fashionably-dressed victims being herded towards a red-painted tumbril waiting by the gates. Their hands were tied behind their backs and the women's hair had been crudely cut short at the back to keep it out of the way of the guillotine's relentless blade.

'I'm beginning to feel like Marie Antoinette . . . ' Barbara murmured in Ian's ear as they were pushed down some worn stone steps into a low, dark vault with cells along both sides.

The vault was lit by flaming torches fixed to iron brackets on the mould-covered walls. Sinister narrow passages led off into the gloom. One of them began as a small room-like alcove which contained a rough wooden table strewn with execution lists. Seated at the table and drinking casually from a large bottle of cognac was the chief gaoler. As they approached, he staggered sleepily to his feet and picked up a huge metal ring loaded with heavy keys.

The gaoler was a short stocky man with ruddy, battered features, black teeth and a huge shapeless red nose. He wore a filthy frock-coat, an open shirt, stained breeches and a pair of collapsed stockings which were full of holes. On his small bullet head was perched a moth-eaten tricorn hat complete with the obligatory tricolour rosette. Without saying a word he slouched over and unlocked a cell door. Two of the prison guards thrust Ian into the cell and the gaoler slammed the door and locked it again. Then he grinned slyly at Susan and Barbara, rattling the key ring in his huge fat hands.

Susan broke away from her escort and ran across to peer through the small window in the door of Ian's cell. 'Ian . . . Oh, Ian . . . ' she cried, tugging uselessly at the lock with her frail fingers.

'Get back, you traitor!' the gaoler snarled, jangling the keys in her face and banging them against the metal lock with sadistic savagery. 'Keep hold of her, you idiots!' he shouted at the guards, hurling Susan back against the wall. He gestured to them to take her down to the other end of the long low vault. As she was dragged away, the gaoler sidled up to Barbara and started whispering confidentially into her ear. 'A lady like yourself shouldn't be kept in a pig-sty like this . . . ' he said slyly, winking suggestively.

Barbara grimaced with disdain and tried to follow Susan and the guards. The gaoler stopped her and jangled his keys.

'Of course, Madame, I have these . . . ' He winked again.

Barbara's face softened a little and she showed a flicker of interest.

'It wouldn't be too difficult to leave a few doors open now would it?' he continued.

Barbara hesitated and then shrugged hopelessly. 'I suppose not. But I'm afraid I have no money. I could not pay you.'

The gaoler edged closer and Barbara forced herself to ignore his bad, drink-sodden breath. 'You see, Madame, the soldiers in this place are no better than peasants,' the ruffian continued in an undertone. 'It gets very lonely for an intelligent man like myself, very lonely indeed.' He slipped his podgy arm round Barbara's waist. 'Now, if we were to be friends . . . ' he breathed, his blubbery lips brushing her ear.

With a cry of revulsion, Barbara struggled free and backed away down the passage. Breathing hard, the gaoler advanced on her once more, arms outstretched and keys rattling menacingly. With a sudden movement, Barbara slashed her assailant across the face with the back of her hand. A ring she wore tore a livid gash in the gaoler's cheek.

He stopped in his tracks, staring at her in disbelief. 'You'll regret doing that, Madame, I promise you . . . ' he snarled savagely. Then he grabbed her arm and propelled her down the passage to join Susan, who had been watching everything in horrified silence in the custody of the guards. 'Lock them away!' the gaoler bellowed, throwing his keys to a soldier. 'No . . . In there!' he added, indicating a narrow, low door round a corner at the end of the vault. 'That's where I accommodate my very *special* guests . . . ' he sneered, making a low bow.

While the soldiers flung the girls into the dungeon, the gaoler wandered back to his alcove, chuckling and dabbing his bleeding face with his sleeve. Throwing himself into his chair, he uncorked the cognac bottle and drank several deep gulps. Then he picked up the sheaf of execution schedules and studied the endless lists of names, his face grinning like a gargoyle in the flickering torchlight.

The door to the dungeon shut with an echoing clang of

doomlike finality. Barbara and Susan gazed around their small dark prison with sinking spirits. A meagre patch of daylight entered through the barred grille high up in one wall, but the dungeon was airless and humid. The rough, flaking walls glistened with condensation and there was a constant drip-drip-drip of water trickling in a narrow stream across the stone floor between drainage holes set at the bottom of opposite walls. Dirty trampled straw covered the rest of the floor. The only furniture was a narrow metal-framed bed with a stinking old flock mattress and a few ragged blankets.

Barbara gasped at the appalling stench of urine and rotten food. 'It reminds me of the last time we were imprisoned . . . in prehistoric times,' she muttered, utterly dejected.

Susan nodded, screwing up her nose in disgust. 'Except there's one important difference,' she said. 'Grandfather and Ian were with us then.'

Susan's manner seemed less downcast, more realistic than Barbara's. She was a little distant, as if she were less affected by their predicament. The teacher glanced enviously at her former pupil, almost resenting Susan's ability to detach herself from the frailty of mere humans at times, however grim the circumstances.

'Perhaps we can see where we are . . . ' Susan suggested, climbing onto the end of the rickety bed and trying to pull herself up by the bars to see out of the grille. 'I can't reach, Barbara. You'll have to help me.'

There was no response. Barbara was standing motionless, lost in her own thoughts.

'Barbara . . . '

'What? Oh, I'm sorry Susan . . . ' Barbara linked her hands and made a kind of stirrup to support Susan's foot.

'I . . . I can't see much . . . ' Susan reported, craning over the ledge. 'Just the courtyard . . . near the ground. The cart's taken those poor people away.'

Barbara sank down on the lumpy mattress and dropped her head in her hands. 'I wish we knew for sure that the Doctor was safe,' she murmured.

Susan jumped down and sat beside her. 'Oh yes,' she said, with a strange smile. 'Yes, he would have got out of the

40

house all right, Barbara. I *know* he would,' she said bravely.

Barbara looked at her optimistic, almost perky expression and smiled bleakly. She squeezed Susan's hand, plainly far from reassured, and tried to work out what on earth to do now.

The Doctor opened his eyes, winced and promptly shut them again. The sunlight was blinding. His ears were filled with the sound of birds. Was he dreaming? Eventually he opened his eyes again, screwing them up against the glare.

Suddenly he was racked by a spasm of nauseous coughing, as if his lungs were turning inside out. His mouth filled with bubbling acid mucus from the huge quantity of smoke he had inhaled and he rolled his head to one side and spat it out. Then he felt his head being gently lifted from the hard ground and a bowl of cool water was put to his lips. He drank gratefully and then coughed up more mucus. Turning aside he spat it out and then greedily drank again until the bowl was empty. With an enormous effort he struggled into a sitting position and blinked his smarting eyes. He found himself face to face with the young peasant boy from the forest, who was kneeling beside him with a frown of deep concern.

'Thank you, my boy . . . Most refreshing . . . ' he croaked, managing a feeble smile.

The boy looked utterly at a loss.

The Doctor grunted at his own stupidity and repeated his thanks, this time in impeccable French. 'And where are my three friends?' he added, glancing anxiously around the deserted farmyard. His eyes took in the smouldering blackened shell of the house and the outbuildings. He sighed and a look of profound despair spread over his severe, pale features.

'The soldiers set fire to the farm,' the boy explained timidly. 'They took your friends to Paris, to the *Conciergerie*. I think they will go to the guillotine, sir.'

The Doctor's nostrils flared ominously. 'The Terror . . . ' he muttered to himself. 'My favourite period.' Throwing back his head he stared down his beaklike nose. 'I see,' he replied gravely. 'You are a very brave boy. How can I ever begin to thank you?'

The Doctor bowed his head and took several deep breaths to clear his lungs. Then he hauled himself unsteadily to his feet.

The boy sprang up and supported the old man's arm. 'There were two men hiding in the house,' he continued. 'One of them knocked you on the head. Then the soldiers came. They killed the two men and arrested your friends.'

The Doctor stared at the burnt-out ruins. 'A tragic business,' he said, shaking his head sadly. 'Who were the two men hiding in there?'

The boy hesitated, as if trying to decide whether to reveal all he knew. Finally he shrugged. 'I can't say, sir.'

The Doctor groaned, suddenly aware of the bad bruising his body had suffered from being dragged down the stairs and across the yard by his plucky little rescuer. 'But you got me out of there,' he said with respectful admiration, ruffling the boy's hair.

'You can still escape, sir,' the boy suggested eagerly. 'My mother will give you food. Our farm's quite near. It's on the way to Paris.'

The Doctor wiped his grimy, sweating face with his handkerchief which was still tightly gripped in his hand. 'Quite right. I must try and rescue my friends.'

The boy's freckled face frowned with alarm. 'No, you mustn't risk that, sir. You'll be caught and sent to the guillotine!' he warned.

The Doctor smiled. 'You saved my life. I must try to save theirs.'

The boy thought for a moment. 'Yes . . . ' he murmured. There was a pause. 'I could go with you,' he said. 'But since my father was taken away . . . He made me promise to look after my mother.'

The Doctor was deeply touched by the boy's courageous honesty. 'So you are the head of the household now, eh?'

The boy picked up the Doctor's walking stick and offered it to him. The Doctor took it. 'Thank you for all you have done,' he said, shaking the boy's scratched and dirty hand. 'What is your name?'

'Jean-Pierre, sir.'

The Doctor nodded and then walked a few steps towards

the gateway. Stopping, he turned and spread his arms vaguely. 'Paris?' he inquired.

The boy pointed past the forest towards the south-east.

The Doctor raised his stick in solemn salute. 'I shall always remember you, Jean-Pierre,' he called, his voice breaking a little. '*Au revoir, mon capitaine.*'

Barbara and Susan lay huddled together on the lumpy, rusty bed apparently asleep. The cover over the spy-hole in the dungeon door slid aside and the gaoler leered lasciviously through at Barbara's shapely figure in the closely-fitting lowcut dress. He watched them for a while, licking his lips and breathing heavily. Then he snapped the spy-hole shut and shuffled away, jangling his keys tauntingly.

'Thank goodness he's gone,' Barbara shuddered, sitting up and loosening the bodice of her dress a little in the oppressive heat.

Susan opened her eyes. 'We'll never get out of this awful place, never,' she said in a hollow voice. 'Not until they come to take us to the guillotine.'

'Now we mustn't just give up like that, Susan,' Barbara retorted sharply in her schoolmistress tone.

Susan sat up abruptly. 'I'm certainly not going to fool myself!' she declared with a trace of desperate smugness.

Barbara tried to smile. 'But think of all the times we've been in danger before. We've always found a way out in the end.'

Susan fixed her large widely-spaced eyes on Barbara. 'Oh yes, we've had our share of luck. But you can't go on and on being lucky,' she objected. 'One day things are bound to catch up with you.'

Barbara gazed at her, shocked and puzzled by the teenager's cold pessimism. 'Susan, I've never heard you talk like this before,' she exclaimed. 'You're usually so . . . well, so optimistic.'

Susan turned away to the wall. 'I just think something awful's happened to Grandfather,' she said. 'It's hopeless.'

Barbara desperately tried to adopt a cheerful air. 'Oh, I'm sure the Doctor's all right, Susan.'

'You keep saying that!' Susan snapped, resentment firing her anxiety. 'I just want to know the truth, that's all.'

Barbara stood up purposefully. 'Susan, we must try to find a way out of here,' she insisted. 'And it hasn't always been luck in the past, you know. We used our initiative.'

Susan grimaced at Barbara's classroom manner and kept quiet.

'Now, we came along the River Seine . . . ' Barbara murmured, turning this way and that as if trying to orientate herself.

Susan snorted with scornful mockery. 'You're surely not suggesting we dig our way out and swim for it?'

Barbara turned on her. 'And why not, Susan Foreman?'

'But the walls are solid stone!'

Ignoring her, Barbara felt around the drainage hole under the window. 'Look how damp the wall is here,' she exclaimed. 'The stone's quite crumbly in places.'

Susan came and peered over Barbara's shoulder. 'That's great. All we need is a couple of pneumatic drills and a gang of navvies.'

Straightening up, Barbara pushed Susan brusquely out of the way and lifted up a corner of the rotting mattress on the bed. 'Well, we'll just have to make do with crowbars instead,' she retorted, tugging at one of the loose iron struts which formed the base of the decaying bed.

'Crowbars?' Susan echoed incredulously.

Barbara nodded in deadly earnest. 'Perhaps we can lever some of the blocks away and make a small hole . . . It might be possible to break into the sewer and eventually reach the river,' she suggested. 'You keep an eye out for that nasty gaoler.'

Susan watched Barbara wrenching at the rusted strut as if she were out of her mind. With a shrug she went over to the door and listened at the spyhole, shaking her head at Barbara's bizarre undertaking.

At last, after an exhausting effort, the determined Barbara managed to work the iron bar free from the frame of the bed. Without pausing to rest, she knelt at the foot of the wall and set to work using the strut as a crowbar to lever out the softened mortar between the huge damp blocks of stone around the drainage hole.

* * *

When he got back to his makeshift office in the alcove of the vault, the gaoler found two soldiers waiting for him with a new prisoner slumped between them like a sack. The prisoner had been shot in the side and his torn and grubby shirt bore a livid dark red patch around the blackened hole. He was moaning pitifully and his dulled blue eyes stared glazedly around as he rolled his head agonisingly from side to side.

The gaoler consulted his stained and crumpled schedules on the table. 'The *Hôtel Conciergerie* is full up. No vacancies . . . ' he chuckled, selecting from his ring the key to Ian's cell and swaggering over to the door. 'He'll have to share with this one.' He peered through the shutter. 'Stand back against the far wall!' he roared at Ian. He unlocked the door and the mortally wounded prisoner was hurled brutally into the cell, screaming out in agony as he collapsed onto the floor. The gaoler locked the door again and banged on the grille with his keys. 'Stop making so much damned noise!' he hissed. 'You'll give the hotel a bad name.' And he shuffled away to have a celebratory drink, chuckling throatily at his own joke.

Ian's cell was larger and cleaner than the dungeon. It contained two beds and there was a largish grilled window in the far wall which admitted quite a lot of daylight.

Ian lifted the wounded man up and carried him as carefully as he could over to one of the beds where he made him as comfortable as possible with pillows and moth-eaten blankets. The man was about his own age, well-built, with fine chiselled features and thick fair hair reaching to his shoulders. His clothes suggested solid bourgeois respectability.

'Make the most of this, old chap . . . ' Ian murmured, putting the rim of his water jug to the man's parched lips. 'This is the last of it, I'm afraid.'

The man drank thirstily and then fell back on the pillows, gritting his teeth and staring at Ian in astonishment, almost as if he had seen a ghost. 'You're . . . You're English . . . ' he gasped, a faint smile cracking his pain-wracked features.

Ian introduced himself.

45

'I'm Webster . . . ' the man croaked, coughing up a mouthful of blood. 'My stomach . . . On fire . . . '

Ian dabbed the man's mouth with a corner of a blanket. 'I think the bleeding's stopped, but you've lost a lot of blood,' he said quietly. 'You must rest.'

Webster closed his eyes. 'Those vermin couldn't wait to pull the trigger on me . . . ' Reaching convulsively for the jug, he fumbled it to his lips and drained it, spilling much of the precious water over himself.

'Maybe I can get you out of here somehow,' Ian said after a pause. 'Escape isn't completely impossible, and you need a doctor.'

Webster folded his weakened arms over his wound. 'It is for me . . . ' he whispered. 'I'll never get up from here.' He lay in silence for a while, shuddering with pain and gasping pitifully for breath. Then he suddenly opened his eyes wide. 'Are you really an Englishman?' he asked, clutching at Ian's hand. 'What are you doing in France?'

Ian mopped the sweat from his face and the blood from his mouth. 'I was going to ask you the same question later,' he said. 'It's a hell of a long story, Webster. Let's just say I'm a traveller.'

Webster tried to sit himself up, his eyes staring wildly with the excruciating effort, but he was getting weaker by the minute and he fell back helplessly. 'I've every reason to disbelieve you . . . ' he muttered, the blood gurgling in his throat. 'But the cards have been dealt now . . . If it's a trap . . . ' His voice trailed into silence.

Ian leaned closer, trying to catch Webster's failing words. 'A trap, Webster? What do you mean? I don't understand.'

The dying man's breath came in convulsive gasps and his face was the colour of chalk. With a gigantic effort he flung his arm round Ian's neck and hauled himself more upright. 'Just listen . . . Listen to me . . . ' he pleaded. 'We know that one day . . . one day soon, France will stop this suicidal madness and . . . and turn her attention across the Channel . . . to England . . . '

Ian nodded encouragingly, supporting Webster in his arms. His mind was filled with a sense of irony that he, Ian

Chesterton, knew from history the truth of what Webster was prophesying.

'England must be ready for that day . . . ' Webster said hoarsely, almost strangling Ian in his fierce determination to convey his important message. 'There is a man here . . . an Englishman in France, working to this end . . . ' Webster struggled on with failing breath. 'He must warn England when that day draws near . . . You understand, Chesterton?' Webster clutched at Ian's shirt collar with his free hand. 'I was sent here to contact the Englishman . . . Take him back . . . The day is near . . . and his information is vitally important . . . Find him, Chesterton . . . Find him and tell him . . . '

Ian almost had to fight Webster off, so fiercely did he cling to him in his death throes. 'I know that France will . . . ' he began.

'Try to escape!' Webster burst out in his face with a last heroic rally of his remaining strength. 'Promise to find James . . . James Stirling . . . To England . . . *Promise* . . . !'

'I do promise,' Ian vowed, flinching at the bubbles of blood frothing out of Webster's chattering teeth. 'I'll find James Stirling and tell him to return to England with his information. I understand, Webster, and I promise.'

Barely alive, Webster released his grasp round Ian's neck and lay in his arms, his breathing now intermittent and shallow.

'But Webster, how shall I find him?' Ian suddenly asked, realising what an impossible thing he had undertaken.

There was a long silence and then Webster opened his eyes for the last time. His lips moved but hardly any sound emerged. Ian bent closer, barely able to distinguish the feeble, breathy words.

'Ask Jules . . . Jules Renan . . . The sign of *Le Chien Gris* . . . ' Ian repeated, watching for some acknowledgement that he had understood Webster correctly.

Webster's lips stopped moving and his mouth hung open. His body gave a brief shudder and his head lolled sideways. Ian gazed sadly at him for a moment and then lowered him gently onto the pillows. He closed the sightless eyes and covered the dead face with the blanket.

4

The Diggers

The Doctor had been walking for several hours through sparse woodlands, across hilly meadows covered in buttercups and long grass and now along a narrow pot-holed road running between tall rough hedgerows. At first he had started off at a lively pace despite the ill effects of his ordeal in the burning farmhouse, but now the heat and the humidity had slowed him down and he frequently stopped to rest on his stick and mop his glistening face. He had shed his frock-coat and slung it over his arm and as he walked he slashed at the hedges to give vent to his irritation and his anxiety about the fate of his granddaughter and her two friends.

Approaching a sharp bend, he noticed a number of crudely repaired patches in the road's stony surface. Rounding the bend, he came upon a small gang of peasants half-heartedly mending yet another pot-hole under the watchful eye of a fat, bullying foreman dressed in ragged trousers, a sleeveless jerkin, calico shirt and a torn straw hat. With his huge black beard and a pistol sticking out of his belt the foreman resembled a pirate captain. He also carried a bulging leather purse on his chubby hip.

'Come on, you layabouts, you can work faster than that,' the foreman was bellowing in his broad country accent.

The Doctor raised his stick in greeting. 'Good day to you,' he cried, his thoroughbred French accent sounding oddly pompous. 'What a pleasant day it is, is it not?'

The gang stopped tinkering with the road and glanced languidly at the cultured stranger. The Doctor nodded and smiled affably. The gang returned reluctantly to their labours.

The foreman screwed up his eyes warily. 'I've seen better,' he growled surlily.

The Doctor smiled again. 'Perhaps you could help me? I am bound for Paris. I take it that I am still on the correct road?'

The foreman pulled a face at the word 'road' and spat into the hedge. 'You are . . . What's left of it,' he replied sullenly.

'Splendid. I was beginning to have my doubts,' the Doctor admitted. 'I haven't seen a soul for hours.' He sighed and sat down on the grassy bank beside the hedge.

Intrigued by the stranger and his unusual clothes, the foreman sat down beside him. 'You've come a long way, Citizen?' he inquired.

'Yes indeed, Citizen. Much further than you can imagine,' the Doctor replied, mopping his brow and loosening his cravat.

The gang had stopped work again and were leaning on their picks and shovels idly scrutinising the Doctor.

The foreman uttered a curse, picked up a flint from the ditch and flung it at them with savage contempt. 'Get on with it. Nobody told you to have a rest!' he roared. He nudged the Doctor, 'You have to watch them all the time,' he complained, his garlicky breath making the Doctor sneeze. 'Can't think why the authorities bother to put them to work. Know what *I'd* do with tax-dodgers, all right.'

The Doctor nodded slowly. 'I see. So they are not voluntary workers, Citizen?'

The foreman guffawed heartily. 'Voluntary? That's a good one. I have to drive them like donkeys,' he snarled, glowering at his men. 'I'm given a schedule . . . Finish this section by tomorrow they told me . . . And if I don't . . . '

The Doctor nodded sympathetically. 'Yes indeed, Citizen. I can see that it is quite a responsibility for you.'

'But it'll be finished on time!' the foreman roared, pulling out the loaded pistol and brandishing it at the gang. 'Even if I have to drive them into the ground.'

The Doctor cleared his throat in the way that he always did when he found himself confronting some particularly

49

irritating aspect of human behaviour. 'I see that you believe in drastic measures,' he muttered, eyeing the resentfully lazy peasants.

The foreman put away the pistol and weighed the bulging pouch in his vast hairy hand. The coins inside chinked pleasingly.

'I am sure you are very experienced in this job, Citizen,' the Doctor said thoughtfully. 'But would you allow an impartial observer to offer you a modest suggestion?'

'I'll take any advice that will get this job done quicker,' growled the foreman.

The Doctor smiled coldly. 'Well, if you were to expend your energy helping with the digging instead of bullying and shouting every few minutes and counting your money, the work would be finished much sooner,' he proposed, rising to his feet. He saluted with his walking stick. 'Good day to you, Citizen.'

The foreman stared open-mouthed at the departing figure, his face filled with outraged astonishment. Then he jumped up and ran in front of the Doctor. 'I suppose you think you're very clever,' he sneered.

The Doctor pursed his lips and frowned. Then he grinned. 'Yes, without false modesty I think I can agree,' he said brightly. 'Now, sir, kindly stand aside.'

With a vicious oath, the foreman whipped the pistol out of his belt and pointed it at the Doctor's head. 'Show me your papers!' he ordered.

The Doctor straightened his shoulders, threw back his head and stared arrogantly down his nose. 'Sir, I am not in the habit of being . . . ' He faltered into silence, realising that he had been caught out.

The fuming foreman dug the pistol into the Doctor's ribcage. 'So you can't prove your identity,' he sneered. 'And have *you* paid *your* taxes, Citizen?' he demanded, bowing with mock courtesy.

The Doctor shrugged helplessly and waved his stick vaguely in the air.

'No? Then perhaps *you* should put *your* energies to better use,' the foreman scoffed, shoving the Doctor in the direction of the watching peasants. 'Now grab a pick and get to work.'

50

With a sigh of resignation the Doctor laid his stick and his coat on the grass and took a pickaxe from one of the gang.

The foreman flourished the pistol under the Doctor's chin. 'And don't try to run away!' he warned.

The Doctor trudged over to the hole and stood staring defiantly at the grinning bully. 'Aggressive fellow . . . ' he muttered. Then he bent over the hole and started to chop away at the broken edges even less energetically than the peasants themselves.

The foreman spat with satisfied smugness and sat down on the bank. 'I'll make that schedule after all,' he grinned, laying the pistol on his knees and unhitching the purse from his belt.

While the Doctor and the road gang sweated away in the hot sun, the foreman sorted and counted his money, occasionally glancing up to bellow at his grumbling slaves.

In the dungeon of the *Conciergerie*, Barbara was doggedly chipping away at the mortar joints between the stone blocks. She was covered in dust and sweat, her arms ached and the palms of her hands were already badly blistered. She had taken a mouldy blanket from the bed to muffle the sound of her frantic excavations, but despite her persistence she had made disappointing progress in the stifling heat. She stopped for a moment to rest her arms and to wipe the sweat out of her eyes. Susan, who was leaning against the door dozing after the sleepless night on the road, opened here eyes at the sudden silence.

'It's no good, Susan, I've just got to have a breather . . . ' Barbara panted, frowning at her painful hands. 'I'm tearing them to pieces . . . and my knees are raw too.'

Susan stirred guiltily. 'Shall I take over again?'

'No, your hands are even worse than mine,' Barbara said firmly.

There was a doomed silence.

'I wonder if Ian's any better off?' Susan sighed, peering through the crack where the spyhole had not closed completely. 'And poor Grandfather . . . '

Barbara hung her head and shrugged, close to defeat.

With a huge effort Susan pulled herself together. 'Give me

the crowbar, Barbara, I'd rather do my stint . . . ' she said. 'There's not so much time to think somehow.'

Barbara got stiffly to her feet and gratefully handed Susan the iron strut. Then she took Susan's place at the door to keep watch. Susan knelt down and jabbed at the wall a few times, wincing at the pain from her blisters. She tried a few more half-hearted jabs and then stuck the end of the bar into the crack and tried to lever the blocks apart. It was quite hopeless. She might as well have tried to fly to the moon.

Susan dropped the crowbar on the flagstones. 'It's no good, Barbara, I just can't . . . ' she whimpered, collapsing onto the bed utterly exhausted.

Barbara came over and slumped down beside her. 'We'll rest for a while and then try again,' she said, endeavouring to sound encouraging. 'We've made a lot of headway already . . . ' She knew it wasn't true, but she felt it was vital not to give in to despair.

Susan suddenly sat bolt upright. 'Someone's coming!'

They listened with bated breath. Shuffling footsteps were approaching along the passage from the vault. Barbara jumped up and grabbed the iron bar to hide it under the mattress. Then she tossed the blankets in a heap against the wall to conceal their modest excavations.

'They're coming for us already!' Susan gasped as the cover scraped aside from the spyhole and a bloodshot eye peered in at them.

Clinging to each other and trembling with cold shivers, they backed away from the door. The key grated in the lock and the door creaked open. The gaoler stooped down and placed two wooden dishes just inside the door. Each dish contained a greyish, glutinous soup, a hunk of stale bread and a wooden spoon.

'*Bon appetit*,' the gaoler scowled. 'Waste of good food if you ask me.'

Susan and Barbara smiled with relief, but they instantly tensed again as the gaoler noticed the pile of blankets against the far wall.

'What are they doing down there?' he demanded angrily.

'What are what doing where?' Barbara asked innocently.

52

'The blankets! I'm responsible for prison property. Pick them up!'

The girls did not budge.

The gaoler leered suggestively at Barbara. 'It can get surprisingly cold in here at night,' he said slyly. 'You need something to make you nice and cosy.' He shuffled across and bent down to pick up the rags.

Susan's fingernails dug deep into Barbara's arm in panic at the prospect of all their effort going to waste if it were found out. But just as the gaoler was about to grab the blankets, a resonant voice suddenly boomed out, echoing dramatically around the cells, the passages and the vault: 'Gaoler? Gaoler . . . How dare you keep me waiting like this. Gaoler!'

'Citizen Lemaître . . . ' the goaler gasped, growing pale and scuttling outside. 'Coming, Citizen!' he called respectfully, hastily locking the dungeon door.

Barbara and Susan listened to his clumsy footsteps vanish into the distance and then hugged each other, almost sobbing with relief at their incredible escape.

'I was sure he was going to find out!' Susan laughed.

Barbara hurried over to pick up the dishes and then they sat side by side on the bed staring at the unappetising grey mush.

'I thought I was hungry,' Barbara groaned, dipping her spoon into the lumpy gruel and letting it drop back into the dish in a series of sticky dollops.

'So did I,' Susan confessed, pulling a face as she tasted a tiny sample from her own dish.

Closing their eyes and holding their breaths, they both forced down a few mouthfuls for the sake of their empty stomachs.

'School dinners . . . ' Susan giggled, covering her mouth.

Barbara swallowed a mouthful the wrong way, choked and sat laughing and trying to swallow at the same time. Susan thumped her on the back and finally Barbara recovered. They sat stirring the foul sludge and bursting into spasmodic giggles like a couple of schoolgirls.

Wiping the tears of hysteria from her eyes, Susan put down her dish and reached under the mattress for the iron bar. 'My turn . . . ' she said, kneeling down by the wall and moving the blankets out of the way.

'No, let me . . . ' Barbara insisted, putting her dish on the floor and blowing on her palms in preparation for the coming ordeal.

She was almost knocked off her feet as Susan suddenly uttered a shrill scream and jumped back from the wall, dropping the crowbar with a clatter.

'What is it Susan?' she gasped.

The dungeon was filled with a furtive scratching and an ominous squeaking sound. Susan's lips moved but no words came out. She shook her head as if in denial of the horror she had uncovered.

Barbara froze. 'What's that noise?'

Susan found her voice at last. 'Rats! They must've smelt the food. They must be in the drain . . . ' she cried, pointing at the small square hole at the bottom of the wall from which the water endlessly trickled.

Barbara reacted quickly. Snatching up the blankets she stuffed them firmly into the hole, blocking it completely.

Susan had scrambled onto the bed. 'It's no good. I'm sorry, Barbara. I can't do any more . . . Not with those things there . . . ' she pleaded, her teeth chattering with fear and loathing.

Barbara tried to comfort her. 'They can't get in here now Susan,' she promised. 'We won't do any more digging anyway. We need to rest.' She sat on the edge of the bed, her face darkening with despair. Then she noticed the two dishes at her feet and a glimmer of hope flickered in her eyes. 'They can't intend to execute us straight away,' she speculated. 'Otherwise, why on earth would they bother to feed us?'

Susan shuddered, her eyes still fixed on the blankets plugging the drain. 'Perhaps they've got something worse than the guillotine waiting for us . . . ' she murmured.

Ian Chesterton had been standing under the barred window in his cell in the hope of finding a breath of fresh air to relieve the foetid heat. At the back of his mind was the anxiety that Webster's corpse would be left where it lay and he shuddered at the thought of what the clammy atmosphere would soon make of it. As he stared up at the hazy blue sky, he almost dreamed of wings and of flight.

The arrival of Lemaître had struck a new fear into him. He vividly recalled the effect the name Lemaître had instantly had on the soldiers in the farmyard as soon as the lieutenant had mentioned it to them. Was this the dreaded interrogator of the revolutionary authorities, Ian wondered, as the gaoler unlocked the cell door to admit Lemaître and then locked it again? He kept his back to the door and waited, his heart pounding and his mouth feeling tacky and dry.

Lemaître was an imposing figure with aristocratic features and a large head. His thick black eyebrows were well-arched, his long roman nose flanked by deep-set chilling eyes. He wore his long black hair tied at the back with a large silk bow, and two long curls swept down in front of his large, sculpted ears. He was dressed in a long black greatcoat with a cape, a frilled white shirt and cravat tied in a bow, black breeches and snowy white stockings. A broad tricolour sash was slung from his shoulder and tied on the opposite hip, again in a large bow. A pair of black gloves and a long thin cane completed the image of austere authority.

He glanced briefly at Ian's back and moved to the bed. Drawing the blanket aside, he gazed with acute disappointment at Webster's dead face. With a sharp twist of the wrist he slashed his cane against his leg in frustration and flung the blanket back over the pale corpse. 'How long has he been dead?' he demanded, his wide nostrils flaring ominously.

Ian suddenly found he could not remember a single word of French. He kept silent, staring fixedly at the sky beyond the grille.

Lemaître strode across, seized his shoulder and whirled him round to face him. 'I asked, how long has he been dead?' he repeated, thrusting Ian hard against the wall.

Ian stared back into the grey eyes, racking his brain for the words.

'Answer me!' Lemaître snarled, raising his cane.

Ian swallowed and took a deep breath. 'Several hours . . . ' he eventually mumbled. 'Citizen.'

Lemaître paused, sizing up this defiant captive. Then he

turned abruptly away and walked slowly round the cell, tapping the head of the cane against his prominent chin. 'Did he speak?' he inquired at last.

Ian thought for a moment. 'No. No, he did not speak,' he replied with calculated hesitation.

Lemaître stopped by the door, deep in some complex inner dilemma, still tapping his chin with the cane. 'What a pity,' he sighed.

Ian waited, tense and afraid, expecting that any moment the strange interrogator would slash him across the face and scream a barrage of questions and accusations.

But Lemaître simply sighed quietly and rapped on the door for the gaoler to let him out. When he had gone, Ian wiped the sweat from his face and sank trembling onto the other bed. He suspected that Citizen Lemaître would be back sooner or later.

Lemaître drew the gaoler across the vault and out of earshot of the cell. 'I shall ask you once more,' he said icily. 'Did they talk to each other? Yes or no?'

The befuddled gaoler licked his lips, uncertain what to say for best. 'Well, Citizen . . .' he mumbled, terrified of saying the wrong thing. 'They may have done . . . But there again they may . . .'

Lemaître's cold stare struck him dumb again.

'Gaoler, just tell me – quite simply – did you ever hear their voices in conversation?' Lemaître asked patiently.

Cornered, the hapless gaoler decided to tell the truth. 'Well, Citizen, yes I did,' he admitted warily.

Lemaître nodded thoughtfully, a trace of a smile playing round the edges of his wide mouth as he walked slowly across the vault to the gaoler's alcove.

Emboldened by the absence of any rebuke, the gaoler trailed after him. 'I didn't hear exactly what they said . . .' he went on, 'but I definitely heard them talking . . . not for long but . . .'

Lemaître spun round sharply. 'Give me the execution lists,' he snapped, sitting in the rickety wooden chair behind the gaoler's table.

The gaoler rummaged through the piles of papers and

handed over several crumpled sheets covered in names.

'This other prisoner, the one in there now . . . ' Lemaître murmured, studying the lists. 'Which one is he?'

Flattered and delighted to be of some use to so grand a personage, the gaoler pointed to Ian's name with his stubby finger. 'That one, Citizen.'

Lemaître's eyebrows arched even more. 'Ian Chesterton . . . ' he exclaimed, a look of surprise briefly flashing across his grave features. He picked up the tattered quill from the inkwell and crossed Ian's name off the list with two bold strokes of the blunted pen. 'Have the body removed from the cell at once,' he ordered, blotting the wet ink.

As the gaoler shuffled off to summon two guards to remove Webster's corpse, Lemaître dropped the execution list on the table and stared thoughtfully at the deleted name. 'Ian Chesterton . . . ' he murmured, tapping his nose with the quill. 'I wonder . . . '

Utterly exhausted, the Doctor leaned on the pick handle and wiped a drop of sweat from the end of his nose. The Time Lord was finding the hot July day unbearably uncomfortable and his hearts were both thumping protestingly as he panted for breath. Beside him the other members of the gang were lazily chipping away at the road without accomplishing anything at all. The Doctor lowered his head and glanced sidelong at the fat foreman who was still sitting on the grass bank counting his money with obsessive concentration. Then he considered for a moment before turning to the peasants.

'Must be the tenth time he's counted that money . . . ' he muttered, roughening his accent a little.

The gang stopped digging and leaned on their picks and shovels. 'Does it all day,' one of them chuckled. 'Likes money more than he likes himself that one.'

The Doctor frowned. 'Any of you lot got any money?' he inquired quietly.

The peasant shook his head and grinned at the others. 'Wouldn't be here if we did.' They all grinned and shook their heads.

The Doctor lowered his voice even more. 'So you'd like to be somewhere else?' he suggested mischievously.

The peasants nodded. 'Fat chance,' said one. 'He's got the pistol and he never turns his back.'

'Just you leave that to me . . . ' murmured the Doctor mysteriously. He spent the next few minutes painstakingly outlining an ingenious plan in as simple terms as possible, while the gang listened like children being told a story.

When the foreman glanced up from his glittering coins he saw that instead of working, his slaves were huddled together staring intently into the sky with shaded eyes. Snatching up his pistol, he shovelled the money back into the purse on his belt and swaggered over to the gang. 'So what's going on? What are you lot gawping at?' he demanded, waving the pistol threateningly in their faces.

'We've just waiting to see the eclipse,' the Doctor explained, exchanging covert nods with a tall thin lad with a gap in his teeth.

The foreman frowned suspiciously. 'Eclipse? What eclipse?'

The tall lad whistled through his missing teeth. 'Didn't you know? The moon's going to pass in front of the sun in a minute,' he declared solemnly.

'Surely you knew about it?' smiled the Doctor.

The ruffian hesitated and then shaded his eyes to peer up at the hazy sun. 'Yes, well, of course I did,' he mumbled disconcertedly.

'It is a most interesting phenomenon,' said the Doctor, pointing upwards. 'It will get almost pitch dark.'

The foreman kept his pistol levelled at them while he scanned the sky for some glimpse of the moon.

'I can see something . . . ' cried the thin youth, raising his skinny arm.

The foreman turned slightly away from the Doctor and squinted even harder.

The Doctor unobtrusively pushed up his shirt sleeve, flexed his fingers and then dipped them deftly into the open neck of the foreman's leather pouch like a conjuror. He closed his fingers around a few coins and skilfully withdrew his hand just as the foreman gave up looking for the invisible moon and glanced back at his workers.

'All right, all right . . . ' growled the foreman. 'We'll see it when it happens. Until then you can all just get back to work!'

He wandered back to the grass bank and sat down again in the shade, still brandishing his pistol. As the peasants reluctantly resumed their toil, the thin lad gaped inquiringly at the Doctor. The Time Lord grinned cheekily and opened his hand revealing several gleaming gold *livres*. The boy's eyes widened in awed admiration. The Doctor bent down and hurriedly buried the coins except for one among the dried clay and broken stones around the edge of the hole. Then he placed the unburied coin by itself on the surface.

Taking up his pickaxe, the Doctor pretended to work away for a minute or so. Then he suddenly stopped. 'Hey, look at this!' he exclaimed excitedly, pointing at the ground.

The road gang gaped at the gold coin and murmured in exaggerated surprise, just as the Doctor had instructed them to. The Doctor stooped, picked up the glittering find and showed it to the gang as they crowded eagerly round him.

With a savage oath the foreman jumped up and strode over to them, flourishing his pistol menacingly. 'What the devil is it now?' he raged, shoving his way through.

The Doctor held up the gold *livre*. 'I just found this!' he said breathlessly. 'It's obviously part of some hoard.' He narrowed his eyes and fixed the foreman with a penetrating stare. 'No doubt the hoard of some tax evader or other . . .'

The foreman snatcehd the coin greedily. 'Hoard?' he scoffed. 'More likely dropped by some passing traveller.' He bit the coin to test its authenticity and his face immediately lit up with avaricious interest. 'Where were you digging?' he demanded.

The Doctor pointed with his pick handle. 'Just there.'

Keeping his pistol trained on them, the foreman thrust the coin into his bulging purse and grabbed the Doctor's pickaxe. Feverishly he started scraping at the place indicated by the Doctor and within a few seconds he had unearthed a second gold *livre* among the clay and stones. 'Here's another!' he roared excitedly, picking it up and testing it in his yellowing teeth before stuffing it into his purse.

'Get your tools, boys. Let's dig!' urged the Doctor.

But the foreman rounded on him, aiming his pistol at the

Doctor's head, his eyes wild with greed. 'This money belongs to the authorities, Citizens . . . ' he declared. 'As their representative *I'll* do the digging. Now stay back!'

Obediently the Doctor led the others aside. The foreman waited until they had retreated to a safe distance. Then he stuck the pistol into his belt, spat on his hands, grabbed the pick and set to work in a renewed frenzy. The Doctor watched for a moment and then winked at the others. Cautiously he took a shovel from the thin lad and edged his way up behind the madly digging ruffian. He hesitated for a few seconds, unhappy about the drastic action he was about to take. Finally he sighed, spat on his hands, lifted the shovel high above his head and brought it down with a clang on the foreman's straw-hatted crown. The big bully uttered a muffled gasp, looked up in almost comical amazement, and pitched forward onto his ugly face in the rubble.

With a nod of satisfaction at his handiwork, the Doctor silently handed the shovel back to the thin lad and hurried over to retrieve his coat from the hedge. While he was putting it on, the peasants suddenly took in what had happened. Cheering their saviour, they flung down their tools and fell upon the spilled *livres* scattered out of the foreman's purse. Filling their ragged pockets with treasure, they took to their heels like children let early out of school.

The Doctor picked up his walking stick and wandered over to the prostrate figure lying in the middle of the road. Kneeling down, he sifted through the rubble and unearthed a buried coin. He polished it on his sleeve and then place it carefully over the foreman's closed eye.

'There you are Citizen,' he chuckled smugly. 'What did I tell you? A total eclipse . . . '

5

Liberty

The screams of terrified prisoners, the yelling of the soldiers and the ominous clanging of cell doors had been growing relentlessly louder and louder. Susan and Barbara sat clinging to one another on the bed in the dungeon, knowing that their turn would come after all. And it did. They heard the stamping of the guards' boots coming round the corner and the terrible grating of the key in the lock. They both felt sick with fear.

'All right, you two. Come on out!' roared the gaoler as the door creaked open.

Prodded by the vicious bayonets they stumbled out into the smoky gloom of the passage.

'Get in line,' the gaoler rapped, locking up the dungeon again.

Susan and Barbara were shoved brutally forward to join the procession of dirty, bleary-eyed, frightened prisoners huddled at the end of the vault. Some were crying hysterically, others simply stared into space as if in a trance.

The gaoler checked the names on his lists against the pale, cowering victims. 'That's the lot for today,' he declared, handing the lists to one of the guards. 'Another batch for Madame Guillotine.'

'But where's Ian?' Susan exclaimed in English, gazing around her.

The gaoler leered cruelly, enjoying her anguish. 'You mean your handsome friend?' he chuckled. 'He was lucky,

Mademoiselle. Citizen Lemaître crossed him off the list.' He leaned forward so that Susan recoiled from his sour alcoholic breath. 'You ladies were not so lucky.'

Susan's eyes brimmed with tears and she bit her lip as if to prevent herself from saying something that might make things worse for Ian. Barbara clasped her hand tightly, her face frozen in a mask of hopeless resignation.

'Take them away!' roared the gaoler, swaggering back to his alcove and his bottle of cognac.

The soldiers drove their victims along the vault like a herd of animals. As they passed Ian's cell, Barbara and Susan caught a brief glimpse of his pale face pressed against the grille in his door, his white knuckles gripping the bars in impotent rage.

'Barbara! Susan!' he shouted, rattling the cell door as if trying to wrench it off its hinges.

The girls tried to stop to speak to him, but they were grabbed and hurled along with the rest of the prisoners up the steps and out into the courtyard.

Ian Chesterton ran across to the barred window and pulled himself up to look outside. He saw a ramshackle cart painted a livid red colour, with a roofless cage of wooden poles lashed together, standing in the courtyard. Between the shafts a dusty old horse stood with sagging knees and drooping head, waiting for its cargo of condemned. He watched with mute horror as the prisoners were herded into the tumbril and the gate was fastened across the back. The bored little driver clambered up onto the box and the creaking tumbril slowly rumbled away escorted by half a dozen soldiers marching raggedly alongside. As the cart turned under the archway and disappeared, Ian caught a heartrending glimpse of Barbara's and Susan's pale faces jammed against the cage and frozen in dulled resignation.

He let go of the bars and slid to the floor. Slumping onto the bed he sank his head into his hands. Up until that moment he had almost managed to convince himself that the whole adventure had been a ghastly nightmare.

Now he knew that it was not.

* * *

Not far from the *Conciergerie*, two young men armed with muskets and shrouded in cloaks despite the heat were lurking in the shadows of a narrow alleyway leading off a forlorn and almost deserted back street.

The elder man was Jules Renan. He had a handsome but slightly fleshy face and his dark eyes were sharp and alert. His short neck made him look stockier than he really was and he wore a flat tricorn hat on his squarish head. His younger companion was very fair and slimmer, with more refined features, and he wore a tall rounded hat with a broad brim. Both men wore their hair tied at the back with small bows. Jules had an air of calm authority, whereas his companion looked impulsive but utterly dedicated to their cause.

'The tumbril should have passed by now, Jules . . . ' muttered the younger man, fidgeting impatiently.

Jules smiled placidly. 'You should try to cultivate a little patience, Jean,' he chided. 'It will stand you in good stead one day.'

Jean tried hard to keep still. 'I shall never ever get used to the endless waiting,' he confessed. 'If only it weren't so stiflingly quiet.'

The air was indeed charged with a feeling of calm before the storm and there were occasional rumbles of thunder over the city.

'That is precisely why we are positioned here, Jean. A crowded street and an ambush do not mix successfully.'

'I know that, Jules, but it's so late. Perhaps they took another route.'

Jules shook his head confidently. 'No, they'll come this way just as they always do. Are you sure you're ready, Jean?'

The younger man checked his musket and the two loaded pistols in his belt. 'I'm ready, my friend. How many soldiers do you think there will be today?' he asked nervously.

Jules smiled to himself. It was a question Jean always asked, like a child needing reassurance. He shrugged. 'The usual: five or six.'

Jean peered out into the street. 'It's a pity Léon cannot be with us today. The odds would have been more favourable.'

Jules Renan thumped his friend encouragingly on the shoulder. 'True. But remember that we have surprise on our side, Jean. That is worth three extra men, *mon brave*!'

The Doctor sat by the roadside on a lopsided block of stone set into the grass verge and half concealed by thorn bushes. He mopped his face and then peered between his knees at the upside down figures carved into the stone.

'Paris . . . Five kilometres,' he panted. Rousing himself with great difficulty, he clambered up the steep bank and parted the tangled hedge with his stick. Shimmering in the late afternoon haze he saw the city of Paris spread out before him like a picture from a history book. He recognised the spires of Notre Dame and the glittering ribbon of the River Seine and in the distance the green foliage of the Bois de Boulogne. But something was missing. The Doctor's eyes narrowed and his nostrils dilated with irrepressible curiosity. That was it! The *Bastille*. The great fortress prison. It was not there!

The Doctor frowned with disappointment. 'Pity . . . ' he muttered. 'I always enjoy the storming of the *Bastille* . . . ' Then he remembered that this was no time for frivolity. Somewhere in that tense and tyrannised city, Susan and Barbara and Ian were in deep trouble.

The Doctor slithered back down onto the road and set off towards Paris with renewed vigour. An hour later he was walking cautiously through the suburbs, keeping as inconspicuous as possible and bracing himself for whatever fate held in store for him in the capital.

Ian was still slumped on the bed in despair when he heard the gaoler clattering around outside with bowls of food and tin jugs of water. The bunch of keys was banged violently against the lock and the gaoler's baleful eye appeared squinting through the grille.

'If you want something to eat you'd better get back against the wall and stay there,' he snarled.

Ian obeyed. The gaoler balanced the bowls on one arm and grasped the handles of several jugs with the same hand as he tried to select the correct key with his free hand while gripping the key ring in his teeth. Eventually he found the key and forced it into the lock. The rusty mechanism squealed horribly as the door opened. Keeping his eyes on Ian, the gaoler placed a bowl of grey mush and a jug of brackish water on the floor and shoved them inside with his foot. Then he slammed the door shut and attempted to lock it, still balancing the other jugs and bowls precariously.

'Gaoler?'

Lemaître's powerful voice rang out so unexpectedly that the inebriated ruffian almost jumped right out of his boots. He fumbled furiously with the jammed lock and struggled to keep hold of all the jugs and bowls.

'Yes, what is it, Citizen?' he shouted nervously, twisting the key with feverish fingers.

Lemaître was standing impassively at the foot of the steps from the courtyard at the end of the vault. 'Come here at once!' he commanded, slashing at the wall with his cane.

The gaoler swore under his breath and fought to turn the key, but the lock seemed completely immovable. 'Coming, Citizen . . . Coming . . . ' he panted, trying to extricate the key from the lock without success.

Lemaître strode towards the alcove. 'Gaoler, I ordered you to come here immediately!'

His cold steely voice seemed to strike terror into the flustered gaoler. Abandoning the jammed key in the lock, the fumbling bully clutched at his overflowing bowls and jugs and scuttled across to his table where Lemaître was waiting for him, his eyes flashing with fury.

'Perhaps you did not hear me calling . . . ?' Lemaître said with menacing sarcasm.

The gaoler dumped the bowls and jugs on the table. 'I'm truly sorry, Citizen,' he burbled. 'I came as fast as I could. I was busy with the food and . . . '

Lemaître's cane cut through the air like a scimitar and sent the bowls and jugs and spoons flying, spilling their unappetising contents all over the walls and floor, 'The prisoners' food is not important!' he hissed.

The gaoler bowed his flea-ridden head in abject submission.

Lemaître stared at him in contemptuous distaste. 'You

realise do you not, goaler, that Citizen Robespierre will be asking to see the weekly execution figures?'

'I have them ready Citizen,' the gaoler mumbled ingratiatingly, rummaging through the mass of papers on the table and wiping off bits of spilt food with his frayed cuff.

Lemaître sat in the chair and studied the schedules with a critical frown. 'I hope for your sake that they are satisfactory,' he warned. 'Otherwise, you might well find *yourself* on the list . . . '

The trembling gaoler hovered anxiously at Lemaître's shoulder, glancing from the execution schedules to Lemaître's noble profile in the hope of seeing some hint as to whether the authorities would consider his quotas to be satisfactory.

As soon as the gaoler had scuttled away, Ian hurried over to the door and stood on tiptoe to try to look through the grille at the outside of the lock. He could just see the end of the jammed key and the iron ring hanging from it. He looked from side to side as far as he could and listened to make sure no-one was nearby. Then he reached through the grille and fiddled cautiously with the end of the key, trying to unjam it. The jangling of the keys at the bottom of the ring made quite a racket and he had to be very careful to work quietly as well as quickly. As a science teacher he knew something about mechanical levers and by gently moving the end of the key around and easing it in and out he was gradually able to free it.

Trembling with excitement, he turned the key to lock the door properly and then removed the key from the lock and lifted the key ring in through the grille. He was delighted to discover that the iron ring had a break in it where keys could be added or replaced. Exerting all his strength, Ian managed to open the ring up just enough to remove the key to his own cell. He put the precious key into the pocket of his breeches and then quickly closed the ring up again by leaning on it against the wall. Finally he selected a key on the ring resembling the one he had removed. Reaching through the grille on tiptoe, he tried to insert the key into the lock. It was very awkward, working blind and with his arm at such an angle between the bars, and several times he almost dropped the entire bunch of keys onto the flagstones.

At last he found the hole and forced the wrong key into the lock, twisting it as hard as he could so that it jammed tight, just as the proper key had done. Wiping the sweat out of his eyes and sighing with relief, Ian picked up the dish of grey gruel and the jug of warm stale water which the gaoler had left on the floor. Throwing himself down on the bed opposite the door, he began to wolf down the cold food with ravenous relish.

Citizen Lemaître rolled up the execution schedules and slipped a tricolour ribbon round them. 'Excellent,' he said with a nod of approval.

The gaoler beamed. 'Thank you, Citizen. My only desire is to serve the cause of the People to the best of my ability.'

Lemaître rose gravely. 'Nevertheless, loyalty should not go unrewarded.' he declared.

The crafty gaoler pulled a face of mock dismay. 'Reward, Citizen?' he protested. 'But I seek no reward.'

Lemaître smiled bleakly. 'That is as it should be,' he murmured thoughtfully. 'But I shall see to it that your name is mentioned in the appropriate quarter.' With a lofty wave of his gloved hand, Lemaître dismissed the grovelling gaoler and strode away.

Grinning with self-importance, the gaoler strutted along the vault checking the cell doors and inspecting the remaining inmates through the spy-holes and grilles. Suddenly his podgy features contorted in horror. His hands flew to his belt where the key ring normally hung. With a whimper of panic he turned and ran back to Ian Chesterton's cell at the other end of the vault. He gasped with relief when he saw the keys still in place in the lock where he had left them. Peering through the grille, he saw the occupant sitting quietly on the bed eating. The thankful gaoler rattled the key to and fro and finally managed to dislodge it. He checked that the door was securely locked and hooked the ring back onto his belt. Puffing out his chest with pride, he swaggered back to his alcove and sat down at the table.

Plucking off his moth-eaten hat, he used it to soak the

sweat off his face and to wipe the gruelly stew from the table. Then he took a fresh bottle of cognac out of the drawer, uncorked it and raised it in a smug toast to himself.

Jules and Jean tightened their grip on their muskets and drew back into the shadows at the mouth of the alleyway as they watched the creaking tumbril shudder to a halt in the narrow street. The old horse stood obstinately between the shafts, refusing to move in spite of the lashing of the driver's whip and the prodding of the escorting soldiers' bayonets. Barbara and Susan stood crushed together with the other prisoners in the back, dodging the fusillade of rotten fruit, eggs, vegetables and other even less pleasant missiles being thrown by the barefoot urchins in the street and by people from their windows along the route to the *Place de la Révolution*.

Eventually a couple of soldiers gathered round one of the nag's back legs, gesticulating and shaking their heads.

'I think they're saying that the horse has thrown a shoe,' Barbara told Susan out of the side of her mouth. 'If they unhitch it, we could try and make a break for it . . . '

Susan looked very queasy after their juddering and unbearably cramped journey in the cart. 'I'm sorry, I don't think I could run . . . I don't feel at all well . . . ' she mumbled tearfully.

Barbara grasped her arm firmly. 'Listen, I'll help you, but you really must make an effort . . . ' she scolded sternly.

They watched the driver clamber down and start unstrapping the harness while the five soldiers stood around leaning on their muskets, arguing and giving advice.

Barbara dodged just in time to avoid a large soggy cabbage that had been hurled from an upstair window.

'I'll do my best,' Susan promised feebly.

'Good girl,' Barbara smiled, just as if she were in the classroom. 'Now, as soon as they start to lead the horse away . . . '

In the alley, Jules Renan peered cautiously round the corner of the wall. 'Trouble with the horse. No wonder they were so late,' he whispered.

Jean nodded, his eyes bright with anticipation. 'There are

only five of them today,' he murmured. 'I'll take the two on the other side of the cart.'

Jules grunted his approval. 'Wait until I give the word.'

As the driver and one of the soldiers dragged the reluctant horse out of the shafts and turned it round, Barbara nudged Susan. 'Ready, Susan?' she whispered. 'I think we can just about squeeze through the bars . . .'

But Susan looked dreadful. Her eyes were glazed and her complexion resembled pale sweaty cheese. 'It's no good,' she moaned. 'I feel awful. I feel sick and I've got a splitting headache. Perhaps it was that nasty food . . .'

'Pull yourself together, Susan Foreman!' Barbara snapped just as if they were in the classroom at Coal Hill School. 'Crouch down and just follow me . . .'

As the soldier and the driver tried to persuade the horse to move away, Jules nodded to Jean. They both broke cover and ran into the street. Jules dropped on one knee, took aim and shot one of the soldiers who was leaning against the tumbril. Jean immediately flung his musket to his friend and whipped out his pistols as he ran round in front of the tumbril. Before the two militiamen on the far side could raise their weapons, Jean shot them and they both dropped like sacks of flour onto the cobbles. But before Jules could aim the second musket properly, the fourth soldier levelled his own gun.

'Look out, Jules!' Jean yelled, distracting the soldier's attention.

Jules flung himself to one side at the same instant as the soldier fired. The ball missed him by millimetres and ricocheted off walls and cobblestones before flying into the fleeing rabble of spectators. Jules took aim and fired and shot the militiamen in the arm. Screaming with pain the man fled in the wake of the terrified, rearing horse and the struggling driver. The fifth soldier came running back down the street, his musket levelled at Jules's head. But Jules just managed to whip out both his pistols and fire and the last soldier fell under the tumbril, mortally wounded.

The prisoners had been so shocked by the unexpected rescue that at first they simply cowered in the cage trying to keep out of the line of fire. But as soon as the shooting stopped they surged forward and broke down the gate at the back of the tumbril. Jumping down, they instantly vanished in all directions in the network of alleyways and back streets.

Barbara held the terrified Susan against her to prevent her being trampled underfoot in the stampede. Jules and Jean ran over and helped them both down onto the cobbles. Unsure who their rescuers were or what would happen to them now, Barbara and Susan let themselves be led away by the two strangers into the bewildering maze of alleys.

Overhead, the thunder trampled sullenly round the sky, as if the forces of some gigantic storm were beginning to gather before unleashing themselves in a cataclysmic upheaval.

Ian had watched the light outside the grilled window fade as black clouds and evening closed over Paris. He had listened to the prison noises fading too. The gaoler had been singing drunkenly for a while but he seemed to have dozed off, succumbing to the effects of alcohol and the insufferably sticky heat. The guards appeared to have abandoned their regular sentry patrols and Ian imagined them dozing at their posts under the heavy humid pall. For him the air was charged with tension and electric excitement. He went over to the door and peered through the grille. The torches flickered smokily, casting oddly flapping shadows across the walls of the long, gloomy vault. Ian took the key out of his pocket and almost caressed it. It was the symbol of freedom and the means to it.

'Gaoler!' he shouted. He listened to the dying echoes and then repeated his call, hoping that he would not get any response. Again the echoes quickly died in the jellified air.

Standing on tiptoe, Ian reached through the grille and poked blindly around the outside of the lock with the key. Eventually he managed to insert it, almost dropping it as he did so. Bathed in sweat, he paused and took a deep breath before twisting it sharply. The lock opened with a click fit to wake the dead. Ian opened the door and crept out of the cell. He closed and locked the door again as quietly as he could and pocketed the key. Then he set off warily along the vault, keeping close to the wall in the shadows. Reaching the gaoler's alcove, he saw that there was nobody there. Beyond the alcove he saw the steps leading to the courtyard and to freedom.

As he started to edge along the wall towards the steps he suddenly stumbled over a large bundle lying in the dark. It was the gaoler's unconscious body.

Bending down, Ian noticed the empty cognac bottle still clutched in his hand and smiled. 'Pleasant dreams . . . ' he murmured in English, scarcely able to believe his good luck so far. He ran lightly to the end of the vault and then up the stairs, hoping against hope that the guards would be in a similar condition to the gaoler.

As Ian ran out into the courtyard, a tall dark figure emerged from one of the narrow passages leading off the vault. It walked slowly across to the alcove and stood over the gaoler's motionless form. A trickle of dried blood which Ian had not noticed lay on the flagstones. It came from a crusted wound on the side of the gaoler's head. Lemaître frowned and wiped the silver handle on his cane with fastidious thoroughness in case there should be any lingering trace of blood on it. Then he stared after the fleeing prisoner, his eyes glittering in the torchlight.

'So, my dear Mr Chesterton,' he said quietly. 'Did Webster give you a message for James Stirling, or did he not? And I wonder where you will go now . . . We shall no doubt find out . . . '

6

Sanctuary

Exhausted and bewildered after their rapid and furtive flight across the Seine and through a maze of streets, Barbara and Susan were ushered into a modest but stylish house whose windows were shrouded behind closed shutters. They were pushed gently but firmly into a dark room where they stood holding each other's hands in silent apprehension, unsure what their kidnappers intended. Jules quickly lit the candles in two large candelabra standing on a polished dining table and the room immediately took on a safe and welcoming appearance. It had a marble fireplace, a sofa and several comfortable easy chairs, besides the wooden chairs around the table. On the panelled walls hung fine oil paintings and heavy brocade curtains were drawn across the long windows.

A young lady appeared and led them to the sofa. She had a pale oval face and was dressed in a long-sleeved frock with lace bodice and cuffs. Over her long ringlets of chestnut hair she wore a frilly mobcap.

'Thank you . . . I'm beginning to feel better already,' Susan murmured, sinking into the soft cushions.

Jules frowned with concern. 'We've closed up most of the house and sent away the servants,' he told Barbara. 'It's safer like this.'

The young lady smiled distantly at Barbara. 'I will bring you some hot soup,' she said, turning to Jean. 'Will you help me Jean?'

When they had left the room, Jules spread his hands in a

typically French gesture of apology. 'It is not exactly a palace, but you are most welcome . . . and safe here.'

Barbara began to relax a little. 'We cannot even begin to thank you . . . ' she said slowly in painstakingly correct French. 'Without your brave rescue we . . . '

Jules spread his hands again. 'Please, I insist that you do not even mention it. That is one of my rules,' he replied kindly but firmly.

Barbara nodded. 'But we do not even know your name.'

Jules looked suddenly very serious. 'We have another rule here,' he told her. 'Christian names only. The less we know about one another the less we can betray under torture. So permit me: I am Jules.'

The door opened and Jean and the young lady entered carrying trays of soup, bread and wine.

'And this is my sister Danielle, and my friend Jean.'

Barbara introduced herself and Susan. Danielle and Jean nodded and bowed.

Jean helped Susan up to the table and they all sat down. Susan and Barbara looked much calmer now and a little colour had returned to Susan's pallid cheeks. They both fell on the thick wholesome soup and the crusty bread with famished enthusiasm.

'After you have eaten you must rest,' Jules advised. 'Tomorrow we shall arrange for you to be smuggled out of France.'

Susan paused, with her silver spoon half-way to her mouth. 'But we cannot leave France. Not yet.'

Jules glanced at Jean and frowned. 'Why ever not?'

'Barbara, tell him about Grandfather,' Susan said, swallowing her spoonful hungrily.

Barbara turned to Jules, almost guilty that she and Susan were safe. 'Yes Jules, we must find the Doctor. And Ian . . . Ian is still in the *Conciergerie*!' she blurted out in a rush.

Unknown to them, the Doctor was at that moment only a few streets away, but of course he also was totally ignorant of their whereabouts. Keeping in the shadows, he walked warily along the darkening streets his eyes darting this way and that, muttering incessantly under his breath as if he were engaged in some tortuous argument with an invisible companion. Earlier, passing the *Place de le Révolution*, he had paused a moment to contemplate the tall macabre silhouette of the guillotine shrouded in its sinister black drapery. Then, with a shudder, he had pressed on with renewed urgency in search of his granddaughter and her friends.

Suddenly he stopped at a corner to peer into a dimly-lit shop window. It was a small, cramped tailor's shop filled with bales of cloth, dummies clad in partly finished garments, and a few rails with finished garments hanging on display. Glancing round to make sure he wasn't being followed, the Doctor went cautiously inside and shut the door.

The tailor looked up sharply from his cutting table strewn with patterns and pieces of fabric. He was a wiry little man with receding hair and a pinched face, wearing a long waist-coat to the knees, rolled-up shirtsleeves and rather thread-bare breeches and stockings. 'Good evening, Citizen . . . ' he said, hastening fawningly across the cluttered shop.

The Doctor nodded and grunted.

'I was just about to close my humble establishment for the night,' the tailor said in his nasal whine, 'but if I can be of service . . . '

'Yes, yes. Quite possibly . . . ' replied the Doctor, examining the garments on the rails with exaggerated care.

'Did you see the executions today, Citizen?' the tailor ventured after a pause.

The Doctor shifted the outfits along the rail with the end of his stick, squinting critically at each one. 'No, Citizen, I did not.'

The tailor watched his customer warily. 'I missed them too, I'm afraid. Most unusual for me,' he added, as though anxious to demonstrate his loyalty to the People's cause. 'Citizen Robespierre is doing a fine job, don't you think, ferreting out traitors and the like?'

The Doctor turned and nodded emphatically. 'Certainly. Yes, the First Deputy is a splendid fellow,' he agreed, fixing the tailor with cold grey eyes. 'I gather that you take an interest in the enemies of the Revolution.'

The tailor hesitated, unsure of the stranger's drift. Then he shrugged. 'I consider it my duty to keep my eyes open, Citizen,' he replied smugly.

'Then perhaps you could confirm that newly arrested suspects are taken to the . . . to the *Conciergerie*?'

The tailor smiled faintly, deciding from the stranger's ignorance and his peculiar clothes that he must be from the provinces. 'That is correct, Citizen. As a matter of fact you can just see the prison from the end of the street.'

The Doctor grunted absently and moved along to examine a different selection of clothes.

'A wise choice, Citizen . . . ' the tailor encouraged him, moving to join the Doctor. 'There is no finer attire in all Paris.'

The Doctor looked neither enthusiatic nor disinterested. 'Oh, I was thinking of a new outfit,' he muttered vaguely. 'Something along these lines perhaps.' He fingered the collar of a smart black coat.

The tailor turned up his nose and stared at the Doctor's dusty garments with frank distaste. 'It would certainly be more suitable than what you are wearing at the moment,' he said acidly.

The Doctor happened to notice a display of impressive sashes and rosettes in the window. 'There are very fine,' he remarked pointing to the largest sashes.

'Yes, Citizen. They signify the office of Provincial Officer . . . '

The Doctor waved his hand impatiently. 'Yes, yes, yes. I'm quite aware of that.' He paused for a moment and then turned and threw back his head. 'In fact that is the position that I myself occupy,' he declared imperiously, flourishing his walking stick and gazing down his nose.

Blinking in awe, the tailor clasped his hands together and squirmed with embarrassment. 'I had no idea, Citizen . . . I apologise most humbly . . . ' he stammered in confusion.

The Doctor smiled frostily. 'No matter, I accept your apology,' he snapped. He picked out one of the sashes and took it over to the smart black coat on the rack. 'I should like to try this on.'

75

'Certainly, Citizen.'

The Doctor removed his own coat, handed it to the tailor and then slipped on the new coat.

'The quality is unmatched, Citizen,' the tailor claimed, brushing the shoulders with his hand. 'And in comparison the price is . . . '

'The price is neither here nor there,' the Doctor brusquely interrupted, 'because I have no money.'

The tailor's smug face fell a mile. 'No money, Citizen?' he exclaimed in a faint voice, his jaw dropping open.

'However, I am sure that a satisfactory exchange can be arranged,' the Doctor added, smiling impudently.

The tailor wrinkled his nose in disgust at the Doctor's old frock-coat. 'Exchange?' he echoed. 'For this?'

'What's wrong with it?' the Doctor demanded.

The tailor shrugged unhappily. 'Well, it's . . . it's little better than a fancy dress outfit . . . ' he protested.

'*Fancy dress*!' the Doctor exploded, his eyes blazing and his mouth turning abruptly down at the corners. 'You'll never see another coat like it!'

The tailor nodded miserably. 'You're telling me!' he muttered under his breath.

'Am I correct to assume that you are not interested?'

The tailor peered at the shabby frock-coat. 'You must understand there is no call for this kind of . . . ' he mumbled, desperate not to lose a customer.

'Have you ever had a similar coat in your shop?' the Doctor challenged him.

'Never.'

The Doctor grinned in triumph. 'Then perhaps that is why there has been no call!' he concluded, slipping the sash over his shoulder and admiring the effect in a tarnished old mirror.

Cringing in defeat, the tailor investigated the frock-coat and its lining. 'Well, it's good heavyweight material I grant you,' he admitted in a conciliatory tone. 'And perhaps with a few alterations . . . ' He glanced up eagerly. 'You are offering to exchange your complete attire, Citizen?'

The Doctor smiled affably. 'Yes, of course,' he agreed, wishing that he had stolen a few of the foreman's gold *livres* himself. A little ready cash would have made things a lot easier for him now.

Still the seedy little tailor hesitated. 'I shall need something else too,' he whined, his eyes lighting on the Doctor's right hand. 'Like that ring for example.'

The Doctor's face hardened into a look of point blank refusal. He examined the ring, turning it round and round on his finger. Finally he tugged it off and proffered it to the tailor. The tailor shot out his grasping little claw, but before he could snatch it the Doctor closed his hand over it. 'You can have the ring provided that you supply me with parchment and writing materials into the bargain,' he insisted.

A suspicious glint came into the tailor's eye, but he nodded eagerly.

'Then we have a bargain, Citizen.' The Doctor handed over the ring.

The tailor grabbed it and studied it closely, while the Doctor hurriedly proceeded to change into his new outfit, unaware of the suspicions he had aroused.

Barbara's and Susan's spirits had rallied after the simple but nourishing meal and a glass or two of wine.

'I do feel better after that,' Susan sighed, sitting back in her chair and smiling at Jules, Jean and Danielle in turn.

'Let me help,' Barbara said, rising as Danielle collected the plates.

'No, Barbara. You need to rest,' Danielle insisted. 'Jean and I can manage.'

As Danielle and Jean carried out the trays, Jules lit a pipe and studied the two young fugitives in the candlelight. In his square-cut tailcoat, high cravat, breeches and stockings, he looked almost aristocratic. 'Now, you both agreed to tell me your story,' he prompted gently.

'What about the map?' Susan reminded him.

Jules smiled and fetched a map from a cabinet drawer. He spread it out on the table in front of them and Barbara and Susan pored over it in silence for a few minutes. The map showed the north-western suburbs of Paris and the countryside immediately surrounding them.

'This could be the forest here,' Barbara suggested eventually, pointing to an extensive patch of green shading.

Susan nodded eagerly. 'Remember we saw a few farms.'

'Turn it this way!' Barbara said, moving the map round. 'There! That would be the forest where we . . .' She glanced at Susan and then turned back to Jules. 'Where we arrived,' she said hesitantly.

Jules stood beside them looking at the map and puffing at his pipe, letting them take their time.

Susan pointed to the map and glanced up at Jules. 'We . . . We were at the edge of the forest and we lost our way . . .' she said lamely.

Both girls hunched over the map again. Barbara traced a road back from the city suburbs towards the forest area, while Susan started from the other direction. 'Yes, we called at this farm!' they chorused at last.

'Oh, I've lost it . . .' Susan murmured as Barbara's bigger hand swept hers aside in the excitement.

'Here! Here's the farm,' Barbara confirmed. 'Here's where the soldiers arrested us . . .'

Jules whipped the pipe out of his mouth. 'Are you sure?' he said sharply, pushing between them and bending more closely over the map.

'Quite sure,' said Susan. 'It was a ruin, really.'

To their astonishment Jules rushed across the room and opened the door. 'Jean!' he called urgently. 'Jean, come here at once!'

'What on earth's wrong?' Barbara murmured, suddenly afraid again.

But Susan jumped to her feet, caught up in the unexpected drama. 'They didn't find Grandfather though. We don't even know if he got out . . .' she gabbled, her words falling over each other. 'Then they set fire to everything . . .' She lapsed into silence, her voice evaporating into a sob.

Barbara had been watching Jules nervously pacing by the door. 'Just a minute, Susan,' she warned, putting a finger to her lips.

Next moment Jean burst in with his hand on the butt of the pistol he carried in his pocket. 'What is it, Jules?' he cried.

Jules seized his arm and led him to the map. 'Barbara, show Jean where you were arrested.'

Barbara pointed to the tiny markings on the map and Jean took a sharp intake of breath and stared at her. Barbara flinched as if expecting to be struck.

'Did you meet two men at the farm?' Jules asked, after a tense pause.

Barbara decided she had no choice but to tell the truth. 'Yes, we did . . . But how did you know?'

'Their names?' Jean demanded.

Barbara thought quickly. She could feel Susan shivering with anxiety beside her. 'I think they were . . . Yes, d'Argenson and . . . '

'Rouvray?' Jules prompted.

Barbara looked up at him in amazement and nodded dumbly.

'Jules, they must have discovered the escape route,' Jean muttered agitatedly.

Jules raised his hand for calm. 'Rouvray and d'Argenson may just have been unlucky,' he warned. 'Do not jump to conclusions until we have spoken to Léon. The route is his responsibility.' He turned to Barbara. 'Were Rouvray and d'Argenson brought with you to Paris?'

Barbara shook her head. 'There was a fight. The soldiers shot them.'

Jean grabbed wildly at Jules's arm. 'This is not the first time . . . ' he snarled, his face dark with fury. 'Somebody must be informing on us.'

'Later, Jean, later,' Jules said firmly.

Susan rose slowly from her chair and stood between them. 'You knew these two men?' she asked sympathetically.

Jules nodded wearily. 'We saved them from the guillotine, just as we saved you and Barbara and the others today,' he sighed. 'Alas, in their case our efforts were wasted.'

'So you have risked your lives before!' Barbara said in a hushed voice, her eyes shining with admiration.

'Many times,' Jean told her, with a look of intense dedication. 'Not all Frenchmen can bear to stand by while innocent people are led to the slaughter. Jules has saved many lives.'

Jules smiled wryly and shrugged. 'It appears that my luck is running out.'

'Luck?' Jean protested. 'Not luck but bravery and self-less . . .'

But Jules would hear no more. Blushing with embarrass-ment he pointed to the door. 'Jean, you must keep watch,' he reminded his hot-headed friend.

Jean nodded and immediately left the room.

Jules sat down at the table and studied the map. 'You say that your grandfather was left here?'

Susan nodded miserably. 'I think he was in the house when the soldiers set fire to it . . . ' she murmured, close to tears again.

'Then I shall send someone to search for him as soon as I can,' Jules promised, grasping her hand reassuringly.

'There are four of us altogether,' Barbara reminded him. 'Ian must still be in the *Conciergerie*.'

Jules gazed earnestly at them. 'I shall not rest until the four of you have been safely reunited,' he vowed solemnly, folding up the map.

All at once Susan moaned and sank back into the chair clutching her forehead.

'Headache?' Barbara asked, concerned.

'Yes, it keeps coming back,' Susan whispered, her face flushed.

Jules went to the door and summoned his sister. 'The young lady needs complete rest,' he told Danielle as she came in.

Danielle took Susan gently by the arm. 'Come with me. You look worn out,' she said.

Susan followed meekly. 'Perhaps if I did lie down for a while . . . '

Jules bowed to Susan and to Barbara. 'Sleep well and have pleasant dreams,' he wished them courteously.

Barbara said goodnight and followed the others upstairs.

When they had gone, Jules sat down and unfolded the map again. He studied it for a long time, puffing silently at his pipe and sending clouds of blue smoke into the candlelight.

The silence was suddenly shattered by a loud knocking at the front door. Jules put down his pipe and ran to the door of the dining room, pulling a pistol from his pocket. Seconds later, Jean burst in also carrying a loaded pistol. At a nod from Jules, Jean ran out into the hall and Jules positioned himself behind the dining room door, pistol cocked and every muscle taut. He heard the front door open and then quickly shut. He sighed with relief when he heard Jean's voice.

'Léon, it's you!'

A resonant voice replied 'I'm sorry to call so late, Jean, but I have a message for Jules.'

The door was pushed open and Léon Colbert entered the room. He was a tall, broad man in his late twenties, with rich reddish hair tied in a ribbon behind his large head. His open, friendly face was not unlike Ian Chesterton's, but his jaw was heavier and his mouth wider. He wore a sombre, striped coat with a high collar and broad lapels, a striped waistcoat, frilled shirt and high cravat.

Jules greeted him warmly. 'Léon! It is good to see you.'

Jean came in behind Léon. 'Rouvray and d'Argenson have been taken,' he announced.

Colbert looked devastated. 'Taken?' he gasped, whirling round to face Jean. 'When did this happen?'

'Later . . . ' Jules insisted, leading Léon to a chair. 'Léon, you have a message for me?'

Colbert wiped his face with a handkerchief. 'There is a man, a stranger, asking for you at the inn, Jules. We are watching him carefully.'

Jules frowned at Jean. 'I am not expecting anyone tonight,' he murmured uneasily.

'Then for heaven's sake be careful,' Leon entreated him. 'Every day we are in greater danger.'

Jules took Jean's arm. 'We'll go to *Le Chien Gris* at once and see what this stranger wants,' he decided.

Jean looked unhappy about the idea but he nodded his agreement. 'Whatever you say, Jules.'

At that moment the door opened and Barbara walked in. She stopped and gave a little cry of disbelief when she saw Léon Colbert sitting there. For a moment she thought it was Ian.

Jules introduced her to Léon and explained her presence.

Barbara swiftly recovered her composure. 'I am pleased to meet you, Léon,' she said, giving him her hand.

Colbert rose and kissed it with gentle gallantry. 'Barbara, the pleasure is entirely mine,' he replied, his dark eyes delving into her with obvious interest.

Jules flashed Colbert a knowing grin. 'Excuse us, Barbara,' he explained. 'Jean and I have to go out for a while. We shall not be away for long.'

Barbara looked rather uneasy, but Colbert took her arm with a brilliant smile. 'I shall take the greatest care of your charming guest, Jules,' he promised, leading Barbara to the sofa.

Jules nodded and he and Jean hurried away into the night.

'Perhaps you would care for some wine, Barbara?' Colbert suggested as soon as the front door had slammed.

Barbara smiled self-consciously and patted a stray hair into place. She felt dirty and tired and very unattractive, but there was something mysterious about the newcomer that excited her curiosity. 'Why not?' she replied. 'Thank you.'

Léon poured them both a glass of *Chateau Barclé*, drew up a chair opposite the sofa and sat down. 'Where do you come from, Barbara?' he inquired. 'Your accent is not Parisian.'

Barbara smiled enigmatically and sipped the warm red wine. 'Does it matter?'

Colbert shrugged. 'No, but I am curious just the same.'

'You may not like my answer,' Barbara replied guardedly. 'I was born in England. That makes us enemies, does it not?'

Léon sipped his wine thoughtfully. 'Does it? I prefer to think that perhaps it means you are not very interested in our Revolution,' he suggested amiably.

Barbara gazed into his magnetic eyes. Something in their depths made her uneasy, but she did her best not to show it. 'Not necessarily,' she said. 'Nobody can deny that it is a historic event.' She laughed nervously and fiddled with her wineglass.

Léon laughed. 'It will be one day,' he agreed, leaning forward so that his face was almost touching hers.

Barbara rose. 'I think perhaps I should go up and see if Susan's all right,' she said.

Colbert rose and watched her leave the room. Then he poured himself more wine and sat staring at the empty sofa and frowning as if he feared that he might have been seen through by a mere English girl.

The *Conciergerie* was silent and dark. The gaoler sat slumped in his chair in the alcove, his tousled, throbbing head swathed in a dirty bandage which sported a patch of dried blood on one side. Among the scattered papers littering the table was a fresh bottle of cognac. He took a hefty swig, banged the bottle back on the table and sank his head in his hands with a profound groan. Whoever had hit him, he decided, had done a good job.

He was roused from his drunken, aching misery by a sudden commotion out in the courtyard. 'Let me in, you incompetent fools! I could have you all guillotined tomorrow!' an angry voice was yelling in a refined Parisian accent. 'Get this gate open at once!'

'Lemaître!' croaked the gaoler, corking the cognac and hastily shoving the bottle out of sight in the drawer. He tried to tidy the papers and clean up the table as he heard the guards shouting to each other and the sound of the main gate being unlocked.

'Thank you, Citizens . . . ' shouted the voice. 'Well, close it again, you imbeciles! Do you want all the prisoners to escape?' A loud guffaw echoed around the courtyard.

The gaoler rose quaking to his feet as the gate slammed shut and he heard brisk footsteps marching down the steps to the vault.

'Who's in command of this establishment?' demanded the impressive figure who suddenly appeared in front of him waving a sheaf of very official-looking documents.

The Doctor was dressed in a smart black coat with epaulettes and a huge tricolour cravat under a stiff wing collar. His breeches were black and his stockings snowy white. On his feet were silver buckled shoes. A huge cloak and a tricolour sash gave him an air of lofty officialdom. But the whole effect was completed by his hat – a tall flat-topped affair with a tricolour band and tassle, and with three enormous white plumes shimmering in the torchlight.

The Doctor slashed at the table with his stick. 'Well? Answer me! Who is in charge here?'

The petrified gaoler gaped in dumb incredulity at the vision. Then he winced and fingered his bloody bandage. 'I . . . I am . . . Citizen . . . ' he finally managed to stammer, clutching the table for support.

The Doctor threw back his head. 'My credentials,' he declared, thrusting the documents into the jailer's numb hand and then striding round the vault peering into cells and checking the doors as if he owned the place, while the bemused gaoler squinted at the ornate handwriting in the gloom. 'And while we're about it, why was I not met?' the Doctor demanded. 'Do you realise that I was obliged to walk through the city unprotected? *Me*!'

The gaoler grinned apologetically. 'We would have arranged an escort if we had been advised . . . '

'You *were* advised!' snapped the Doctor. 'I forwarded the communication myself. If Citizen Robespierre should hear about this appalling lapse . . . '

At the mention of the dreaded name the gaoler turned green. 'Citizen Robespierre?' Oh, I don't think you should bother him with it . . . ' he mumbled, sidling up to the awesome visitor. 'He's a very busy man these days . . . '

'So am I!' thundered the Doctor.

The gaoler handed back the documents with a bow. 'I am entirely at your service, Citizen,' he said. 'I will be happy to oblige you in any way.'

The Doctor stared disdainfully at the obsequious figure and permitted himself a faint smile. 'Very well. You seem a capable man,' he said kindly. 'I am sure you were not responsible for the misunderstanding.'

The gaoler squirmed and wrung his hands. 'Oh indeed, Citizen. I am most conscientious, but when one is assisted by idiots . . . '

The Doctor nodded, the plumes in his hat waving majestically over his head. 'Quite. I see we understand one another.'

The gaoler's bloated face puffed into a broad grin as he congratulated himself on pacifying the important official. He pulled up a chair for his distinguished visitor. 'A little cognac, Citizen?' he inquired.

'No, thank you,' said the Doctor, sitting down.

But the gaoler picked up a mug, wiped it out with his elbow and set it in front of the Doctor. Then he took out the bottle and poured him a generous measure. 'Citizen, I would deem it a privilege if I could be of help,' he said, plonking himself in the other chair.

The Doctor bowed his head in acknowledgement. 'It is a simple matter,' he explained. 'Three traitors were arrested in my province and brought here – a young man, a young woman and a girl. I wish to interrogate them.'

The gaoler's smug grin instantly evaporated. He stopped with the bottle half-way to his lips. 'The two women were dispatched to the guillotine yesterday, Citizen,' he said.

The Doctor quickly turned away his head so that the ruffian would not see his devastated reaction.

There was an ominous pause. The the gaoler cleared his throat. 'Unfortunately . . . there was a rescue, Citizen,' he finally confessed.

The Doctor turned sharply. 'Rescue? By whom?'

The gaoler took a couple of fortifying swigs of cognac. 'We don't know yet. It's happened a lot recently. You realise I'm not to blame, Citizen,' he added nervously. 'Once the prisoners leave the *Conciergerie* they're outside my jurisdiction.

The Doctor waved his hand impatiently. 'Yes, yes, of course, of course . . . But what about the young man?'

The gaoler squirmed uncomfortably. 'The young man, Citizen?' he stalled.

'Come on, out with it!' snapped the Doctor.

'He escaped too, Citizen.' The unhappy gaoler pointed to his bandaged head. 'He was a dangerous fanatic. He almost killed me. I fought with him. I was ready to sacrifice my life to prevent his escape . . . But he fought like ten men . . . '

The Doctor rose gravely to his feet. 'I believe you, Citizen. You did all you could,' he said. 'It would never have happened were you not surrounded by incompetent fools.'

The gaoler staggered to his feet nodding vehemently.

The Doctor paced to and fro. 'So, the three of them are at liberty, somewhere in Paris . . . ' he mused.

The gaoler sidled unsteadily over to him. 'They'll be caught Citizen, rest assured,' he promised.

'What? Oh yes. Thank you, Citizen,' said the Doctor absently, picking up his stick and his papers from the table and turning to depart. 'I shall take up no more of your time.'

As he did so, a tall figure stepped out of the narrow passage leading off the alcove. It was Lemaître. The Doctor hesitated, staring at the imposing figure, uncertain what to do.

The gaoler scuttled over to Lemaître. 'Citizen Lemaître, the Citizen here has been inquiring . . . '

Lemaître waved him away. 'I heard what was said,' he snapped, gazing intently at the Doctor as though trying to fathom the true purpose behind the stranger's inscrutable grey eyes. 'Your papers, Citizen!' he demanded.

The Doctor handed over his documents and Lemaître flicked open the folded papers as if he were swatting a fly.

'The Citizen is a Provincial . . . '

'I can read, thank you, gaoler,' Lemaître retorted caustically, scanning the documents impassively. He handed them back to the Doctor. 'Where you you going now, Citizen?' he demanded.

The Doctor smiled unflinchingly. 'Back home, Citizen.'

Lemaître smiled back and they stood face to face in silence for a moment. 'It is rather late. Perhaps you should postpone your journey until tomorrow,' he suggested.

The Doctor hesitated and then shrugged. 'Why yes, I suppose I could,' he agreed.

'You see, I shall be taking the execution reports to the First Deputy,' Lemaître went on. 'By a happy coincidence your province is to be discussed. Your presence would be a great advantage . . . You would be on hand to answer any queries that may arise.'

The Doctor was trapped. He had no choice but to agree. 'What a good idea,' he smiled.

'I promise you will find it most interesting,' Lemaître said, taking the Doctor's elbow. 'Come, Citizen, we must not keep First Deputy Robespierre waiting, must we!'

Resigning himself to the inevitable, the Doctor allowed Lemaître to lead him away, his mind a turmoil of anxiety about the fate of Susan and their two friends and about what kind of bluff he would manage in front of the Tyrant of France himself.

Not long after Lemaître and the Doctor had left the *Conciergerie*, another visitor hammered at the prison gates demanding to be admitted on important business. Eventually he was let in and taken to the alcove in the vault, where the gaoler was slumped over his bottle of cognac. There he asked to see the Provincial Officer.

'He's not here,' the gaoler retorted in a surly tone. 'He's gone to visit Robespierre with Citizen Lemaître. Anyway, what's it all about?'

The visitor held up something in his fingers.

The gaoler peered shortsightedly at the gleaming object. 'What is it?' he growled.

The visitor grinned slyly. 'Evidence, Citizen Gaoler. Evidence against a traitor.'

The visitor was the tailor. He was holding up the Doctor's ring and his beady eyes were glittering with venomous spite.

7

The Tyrant of France

Maximilien Marie Robespierre, First Deputy of the Convention, had just returned from a violent and terrifying meeting at the Jacobin Club where he had made a two hour speech demanding a purge of the Committee of Public Safety. His speech was a repeat of the one he had made the previous afternoon in the Convention itself – the governing assembly of the Revolution. Utterly exhausted, he slumped at his desk shuffling papers and staring wildly around as if he suspected assassins in every shadow.

He was a small, thin man of thirty-two. His hair was carefully brushed back and powdered, but his complexion was pasty and pock-marked. His skin had a sickly greenish tinge and his short-sighted eyes were also green. A nervous tic frequently convulsed the side of his face, drawing the corner of his thin-lipped mouth up towards his ear. He dressed with fastidious care, wearing a blue nankeen tail-coat, striped blue waistcoat, a red and white striped cravat, and white silk breeches and stockings. On his tiny feet he wore high-heeled buckled shoes in a vain attempt to increase his meagre stature. To many he looked more like a survivor from the court of the executed King Louis XVI than the most feared and radical revolutionary: the Tyrant of France.

He looked up sharply as Lemaître ushered the Doctor into his ornate high-ceilinged chamber.

Lemaître presented to him the execution lists from the *Conciergerie* and the other prisons. 'Here is the complete and detailed schedule of recent executions, Citizen,' he said respectfully.

Robespierre gave the papers a cursory glance and then screwed up his eyes at the Doctor. 'Who is this?' he inquired in his weak voice, his face twitching.

Lemaître motioned the Doctor forward. 'A visiting Provincial Deputy from Pontoise,' he explained. 'As the region is to be discussed, I thought the Citizen should make his report to you personally.'

Robespierre blinked coldly at the Doctor. 'There are more vital matters to consider,' he whined. 'However I am always prepared to receive news of the provinces.' He gestured to the Doctor to take a seat in the chipped gilt chair opposite him.

Lemaître remained standing behind the chair.

'I welcome the opportunity,' the Doctor said with a slight bow. 'But before I report on Pontoise, perhaps the First Deputy would care to hear my impressions of the capital itself?'

Robespierre raised his thin eyebrows in surprise. 'When did you arrive in Paris?'

'Early yesterday.'

Robespierre waggled his waxen fingers. 'Hardly sufficient time for you to assess the present mood of the capital!' he objected.

The Doctor shrugged. 'I wouldn't say that. I have the distinct impression that the mood in Paris has turned violently against . . . '

Robespierre rapped the desk with his knuckles. 'I am interested only in your report on your province, Citizen!' he snapped. 'Now, recent intelligence suggests that the purging of our enemies there has been progressing extremely slowly.'

The Doctor looked very surprised. 'Indeed, Citizen?' he retorted. 'Well, perhaps that is because we have fewer enemies of the Revolution in Pontoise.' He grinned complacently. 'Perhaps Paris can learn something from us simple country folk.'

Behind him, Lemaître breathed in sharply as though warning him to take care.

Robespierre sprang out of his chair and walked rapidly around the room. 'We in Paris are perfectly well aware of the dangers,' he proclaimed. 'We live in troubled times. There is much work to be done. Work that is constantly delayed by the need to ferret out the traitors we harbour in our midst.'

The Doctor bristled visibly at the tyrant's claim. 'Is there really such a need?' he argued. 'What can your Reign of Terror possibly accomplish? Traitors are like weeds. For every one you guillotine two more will spring up again.'

Lemaître bent forward and spoke quietly into the Doctor's ear. 'I think you have said quite enough, Citizen,' he warned.

'Oh, you do, do you?' cried the Doctor, thoroughly aroused.

Robespierre clapped his hands. 'Let him speak. What he says is true. My enemies do multiply. He is only reminding me of the dangers I face – even in the Convention and the Committee of Public Safety.'

Lemaître bowed and stepped back a pace as Robespierre stopped in front of the Doctor.

'I shall achieve great things for France,' Robespierre declared grandly. 'For too long the Monarchy and Church and the Nobility kept the People under their thumbs. Now the way forward is clear . . . But what happens? My colleagues, my most trusted friends resent me and plot for power behind my back.'

The Doctor could not resist rising to the argument. His eyes gleamed and his voice rang out authoritatively. 'Do they?' he wondered. 'Or do they perhaps merely desire to keep their heads?'

Unaccustomed to such confrontrations, Robespierre stared silently at the Doctor for a while and then abruptly resumed his furious pacing. 'Danton plotted to restore the Monarchy . . . ' he raged, his greenish eyes ablaze with malevolent fanaticism. 'I had to remove him. And the Girondins . . . And even as we speak I know that Convention members are plotting my downfall. But I shall triumph, even if I have to execute every single one of them.' Robespierre's voice rose almost to a shriek. 'Death . . . Always death . . . Do you think I *want* this carnage to go on and on?' He snatched up several documents from the desk and thrust them at the startled Doctor. 'Three hundred and forty-two executions in nine days in Paris alone . . . ' he cried almost hysterically. He went over to the shuttered window and peered through a narrow crack into the darkness. Then he returned to sit at the desk, burying his head in his hands in despair. 'What a legacy I shall leave behind me if this slaughter has to continue . . . ' he groaned almost inaudibly.

The Doctor opened his mouth to pursue the debate, but Lemaître's hand on his shoulder silenced him. He replaced the documents on the desk and followed Lemaître to the door in silence.

Robespierre looked up. 'You must come and see me again, Citizen,' he suggested wearily. 'We never did discuss the situation in Pontoise, did we?'

The Doctor turned in the doorway. 'What a pity, no . . . ' he replied, catching a look from Lemaître that told him the fellow realised he had sidetracked the matter of the province and its affairs deliberately. 'I was quite looking forward to it,' he lied, flashing Lemaître a winning smile.

'Bring him with you tomorrow, Lemaître,' Robespierre instructed, bending over his papers.

The Doctor's smile instantly vanished.

'Of course, Citizen Robespierre,' Lemaître replied. It was his turn to smile at the Doctor. 'Until tomorrow then . . . '

Huddled in a blanket despite the hot, close night, Susan sat in an armchair shivering as if she had a fever. Barbara was kneeling anxiously beside her holding her hands, while Léon Colbert stood with his back to the empty fireplace with an enigmatic smile on his face, fascinated by the two puzzling guests.

Danielle brought in a glass of brandy. 'Here, Susan, this will make you relax,' she said kindly.

Susan stared suspiciously at the glass. 'What is it?'

'Just drink it all up,' Danielle encouraged her.

Susan glanced warily at Barbara, who nodded reassuringly. She drained the glass and coughed as the raw spirits scorched her throat.

'I should like some more wine,' said Léon.

Danielle pointed to the tray on the dining table without looking at him.

Colbert smiled. 'Why, thank you, Danielle,' he said with mock politeness.

Jules's sister turned to Barbara. 'I think I shall return to bed now, if you will both excuse me,' she said quietly.

Barbara nodded. 'Thank you, Danielle. I'm sorry we disturbed you.'

Danielle glanced momentarily at Colbert's challenging smile then tossed her head contemptuously and hurried out.

Léon shrugged and helped himself to more wine. 'One cannot be friends with everyone,' he sighed languidly.

Barbara tucked the blanket more securely round Susan. 'Try to get some sleep,' she advised. 'I'll be here if you need me.' Susan closed her eyes and let the brandy lull her into a doze.

Barbara moved across to the fireplace. 'I wish I knew what was wrong, Léon. She could have caught something quite serious in that dungeon.'

He shrugged. 'Probably just a chill.'

'But what if *is* something serious?'

Léon sipped his wine and considered. 'We could call a physician, but it is risky. People report every small occurrence to the authorities these days, just to be sure of saving their own skins.'

Barbara watched Susan's glistening forehead and her rapid shallow breathing. 'It is a chance we must take,' she decided. 'Léon, you must know a physician we can trust.'

Colbert looked full of admiration for Barbara's resolution. 'Yes, I think I do.' He drained his glass. 'But it may take a little time to find a reliable man. I wonder where Jules and Jean have gone? They should have returned by now.'

Barbara grasped his arm. 'Léon, we shall be quite safe here,' she said earnestly, hinting that he should be off in search of a doctor.

Léon looked at her and for a moment she thought he was about to seize her and kiss her passionately. But the moment passed. 'If I am not able to return myself I will send a message,' he said, moving to the door. 'You'll tell Jules?'

'I'll tell him. Be careful, Léon.'

Colbert paused in the doorway. Again he seemed to be on the brink of rushing across to embrace her like a young blood out of an adventure story. 'Do not worry about me, Barbara,' he said quietly. 'We shall meet again. And soon.'

As soon as he had departed, Susan stirred under the blanket and opened her eyes.

'I thought you were asleep,' Barbara exclaimed in surprise, taking one of the candelabra from the table. 'Come on, I'll help you back to bed.'

'You like that Léon, don't you?' Susan murmured, a hint of mischief in her voice in spite of her feeling so unwell.

Barbara smiled secretively and shrugged and led Susan back upstairs.

Some time later, the shutters were suddenly thrown aside and the long dining room windows were opened from outside. Jean backed into the room carrying one end of a body, its head wrapped up in sacking. Jules Renan followed struggling with the other end. They laid their heavy burden on the sofa and Jules hurried to close the shutters and the windows again.

'Now, let's have a proper look at him . . . ' Jules panted, wiping his face with his sleeve. 'I hope you didn't hit him too hard, Jean.'

Jean brought the remaining candelabra over to the sofa. 'It was the only thing I could do, with all the militiamen about,' he said. 'If he had made the slightest move we could all have been arrested. It might have been a trap.'

Jules lifted the sacking. 'I wonder who he is . . . ' he muttered.

In the flickering candlelight they gazed down at the pale unconscious face of Ian Chesterton.

'No, Citizen, I should say you made a most favourable impression on the First Deputy,' Lemaître told the Doctor as they walked across the courtyard of the *Conciergerie* and down the steps into the cell vault.

The Doctor shook his head in disappointment. 'But I didn't manage to say half the things I wanted to say,' he complained bitterly. 'Citizen Robespierre simply twisted my words around.'

Lemaître spread his arms in a French shrug. 'Politicians usually do,' he smiled. 'Still, you shall have another opportunity tomorrow.'

The Doctor pulled a face. 'Oh, I think not, Citizen. I fear that I must take my leave and return home after all.'

Lemaître took his arm firmly. 'But that will be rather awkward, Citizen,' he pointed out. 'Robespierre will be expecting you.'

The Doctor tugged himself free. 'Well, you'll just have to convey my sincere apologies to him . . . ' he said regretfully.

'On the contrary,' Lemaître butted in. 'That would be more than my neck is worth. You must stay.'

The Doctor stopped by the gaoler's alcove, threw back his head and smiled his strange, rather frightening half-smile with the corners of his mouth turned down. 'Out of the question, I'm afraid.'

Lemaître moved quickly round to cut off the Doctor's escape. 'But I insist!' he murmured.

They stood nose to nose for several seconds in a head-on confrontration. Then the Doctor gradually backed down and turned away with a weary sigh.

'Gaoler!' Lemaître shouted impatiently.

The gaoler had been snoring raucously in a drink-sodden stupor. He snorted himself abruptly awake, dragged his head up off the table and blinked at the shadows. 'What's the . . . Citizen Lemaître!' he gasped.

'Arrange suitable accommodation for our guest from the provinces,' Lemaître ordered.

Clutching his throbbing head, still swathed in its bloody bandage, the gaoler jumped up. 'At once, Citizen. For how long?'

'He will be staying at least until tomorrow.'

'Definitely no longer,' the Doctor snapped, folding his arms and drawing the capacious cloak more closely around him despite the heat.

The gaoler unhitched his keys from his belt. The Doctor's high forehead furrowed suspiciously and his eyes narrowed. Perhaps he would have to make a break for it after all.

'He can have one of the guards' rooms . . . ' yawned the gaoler. 'I'll turn the layabouts out.'

The Doctor breathed more easily again. At least he was not going to be locked up. Or was he?

The gaoler scratched himself shamelessly. 'I forgot, Citizen. There's a man been waiting to see you,' he told Lemaître. 'Says it's very important. He's waiting in your room.'

Lemaître excused himself. 'I trust you will find your room satisfactory,' he told the Doctor, before nodding and striding away along the narrow passage leading off the alcove.

The Doctor stared impassively after him. 'I am sure I shall have no cause for complaint, Citizen . . . '

The gaoler sniffed, spat, wiped his nose on his sleeve and jerked his thumb at the Doctor to follow him. 'I'll show you to your room,' he growled with affected courtesy.

Glancing along the passage to make sure Lemaître had gone, the Doctor grabbed the gaoler's arm. 'Don't trouble yourself, gaoler. I've changed my mind. I shan't be staying after all,' he said quietly. 'Citizen Lemaître will understand. I really shouldn't have insisted he put me up overnight. Besides, the soldiers need their rest.'

'Don't matter about them,' mumbled the gaoler, hesitating.

The Doctor raised his hand. 'Nevertheless, I really must be on my way. I have a long journey ahead of me. Give Citizen Lemaître my sincerest regards.'

The gaoler watched the Doctor start striding towards the steps to the courtyard. Then he snatched open the drawer and whipped out a loaded pistol. 'Citizen!' he cried, levelling it at the Doctor's head. 'Lemaître said you were to stay. I must obey him.'

The white plumes in the Doctor's tall hat quivered with outrage. 'You dare to threaten me!' he breathed, stopping in his tracks. 'What do you think Citizen Lemaître will say when he hears about your behaviour?'

The gaoler shrugged miserably. 'I'm sorry, Citizen, but if he finds you've gone it could be even worse for me,' he whined.

The Doctor considered a moment and then shook his head

95

in defeat. 'Very well, I shall stay . . . ' he conceded. 'And I shall say nothing of this disgraceful exhibition, since it is not your fault.'

The gaoler grinned hideously. 'Thank you, Citizen, thank you.' He stuck the pistol into his belt. 'Please come this way.'

Clearing his throat dramatically, the Doctor strode off in the direction of the guards' quarters, leaving the drunken buffoon to scamper after him like a sleepy dog.

Lemaître's room was a small, bare, cell-like place with stone walls and floor, furnished only with a table and two wooden chairs. A pair of guttering candles provided the only illumination. Lemaître sat in one chair examining the ring which his visitor had given him. The tailor sat in the other chair, dry-mouthed and nervous in the presence of so important an official.

After a long silence Lemaître sat back, idly toying with the ring. 'So you claim that the white-haired old gentleman exchanged his clothes and this ring and that you also provided him with writing materials?' he asked coldly.

'Don't forget the sash, Citizen,' mumbled the tailor. 'It was the Provincial Official Sash that really aroused my suspicions.'

'Yes indeed,' Lemaître nodded patronisingly.

The tailor squirmed hesitantly in his chair. 'Of course, I realise it may be nothing. I may be mistaken. But I felt it was my duty to report the incident.'

Lemaître smiled faintly. 'Indeed, you have done well, Citizen.'

The tailor's pinched features clouded with disappointment as it dawned on him that he was unlikely to be rewarded for his information. He got slowly to his feet, assuming that the interview was over. Plucking up his meagre courage, he coughed quietly. 'Will . . . will you be keeping the ring, Citizen?' he inquired, loathe to depart empty-handed.

'It may be required as evidence,' Lemaître replied, pre-occupied

'Only it was part of our bargain, Citizen. The clothes he gave me in exchange were almost worthless,' the tailor lied.

'I'm just a poor man, Citizen, otherwise I'd have thrown the scoundrel out of my shop.'

Lemaître dipped his hand into his coat and pulled out several gold *livres*. 'Here, this should more than compensate you.'

The scrawny little man grinned craftily. 'Thank you, but I cannot accept any reward, Citizen. I only did my duty.'

Lemaître saw through the feeble deception. 'Keep it,' he insisted. 'But on one condition . . . You will say nothing of this matter to anyone.'

'You have my word, Citizen,' the tailor smiled, thrusting his reward into his pocket.

Lemaître rose and opened a second door in the opposite wall. 'Go this way,' he ordered. 'I don't want our so-called Provincial Officer to see you.'

The tailor scuttled out into the courtyard. Lemaître locked the door behind him and sat down to study the ring again, turning it over and over in his hands and frowning with dark suspicion.

Jules and Jean had sat Ian upright on the sofa and had been anxiously waiting for the stranger to show some sign of life.

Eventually Barbara came in, looking extremely worried.

'Sorry we were away so long,' Jules said with a wry smile. 'We had to dodge all the patrols. How is Susan?'

'She's feverish, but she's sleeping now,' Barbara replied. 'Léon had to leave. He offered to find a physician for Susan.'

Jules nodded his approval.

Ian's eyes flickered open, as if at the familiar sound of Barbara's voice. He groaned and clutched his head and tried to sit up, but the effort defeated him and he sank back onto the cushions.

Barbara moved closer to the sofa. When she recognised Ian she almost fainted wth astonishment and relief. 'Ian . . . Ian, you're safe!' she cried, kneeling in front of him and taking him tenderly by the shoulders.

Jules and Jean exchanged puzzled glances as Ian stared at Barbara in confusion and then reacted with a joyful smile.

'Barbara . . . ' he muttered, getting shakily to his feet and raising her up in his arms. 'Thank God, you're all right. And Susan? Is she here?'

Barbara nodded. 'Asleep upstairs.'

'This is just great!' Ian grinned. Then he winced at the dull ache in his head. 'I was convinced you were both . . . Any news of the Doctor?'

Barbara frowned gloomily. 'I'm afraid not. We don't even know if he reached Paris.'

The two Frenchmen moved closer, unable to understand the conversation in English.

'Well, Barbara, when we left we had no idea we were going to meet one of your friends,' Jules laughed.

Barbara introduced Ian to them in French. 'This is Ian Chesterton. Ian, this is Jean and this is Jules Renan. Susan and I owe our lives to them.'

Ian stared at Jules in amazement. 'Jules Renan? I have been searching for you,' he said softly in his halting French.

'If only we had known who you were . . . ' Jules apologised, gesturing at Ian's head.

Ian massaged his thudding temples. 'Never mind, Jules. You have reunited me with my friends.'

Jules turned to Jean. 'This calls for a celebration. Bring a fresh bottle from the cellar.'

Barbara moved to the door behind Jean. 'I'll go up and sit with Susan,' she told Ian. 'She's not at all well. We hope to get her to a doctor tomorrow, though when she hears that you're safe it should do more than any medicine for her.'

Barbara left the room and Ian sat down heavily on the sofa still feeling very groggy, though he actually looked a lot better.

Jules put his pipe in his mouth without lighting it. 'I have a question,' he said. 'How did you know Barbara and Susan were here?'

'I did not know. I am amazed,' Ian replied.

Jules gazed at Ian. 'But you were asking for me, for Jules Renan . . . Why?'

Ian struggled to gather his thoughts into some reasonable order. 'Do you know a man called Webster?' he asked after a long silence.

Jules pondered a moment. 'No, I do not.'

'We shared a cell in the *Conciergerie*,' Ian explained. 'Unfortunately he died, but before that he asked me to contact a James Stirling.'

Again Jules pondered. 'James Stirling?' He shook his head regretfully. 'I am sorry, but that name means nothing to me either.'

Ian's face fell in bitter disappointment. 'So you do not know him . . .'

'Should I?' Jules shrugged.

'I am not sure,' Ian murmured weakly. 'I just took it for granted that you would.'

At that moment Jean returned with a bottle of wine and fresh glasses. 'I will share one glass and then I must leave on my journey,' he said to Jules as he poured out the wine.

Jules nodded discreetly.

They raised their glasses in silent mutual toast.

'I think you should tell your whole story,' Jules suggested.

Ian took a deep breath. 'Well, as far as I could gather, this man Webster – he was English – had been sent over here to instruct James Stirling to return to England. Stirling is . . . well, he is some kind of spy. Webster and I ended up in the same cell in the *Conciergerie* and he was dying . . . He begged me to contact Stirling for him. I asked Webster how I could find Stirling, but he was already so weak that he could hardly speak . . . All he said was that I should look for Jules Renan at the sign of *Le Chien Gris*.'

A long silence followed the Englishman's strange tale.

'I see,' Jean murmured, glancing at Jules. 'Webster was right, *Le Chien Gris* is an inn we frequent.'

'Did Webster know Stirling?' asked Jules.

Ian shrugged. 'I suppose he must have.'

Jules paced around the room. 'If Stirling is a spy he must be able to move around freely to do his job successfully . . . That would require an alias . . . a completely new identity.'

'Which perhaps Webster did *not* know,' Ian added. 'So Webster was counting on being able to recognise Stirling.'

Jules sighed and sipped his wine. 'It is a good *theory*, Ian.'

'But why did he give me *your* name?' Ian wondered.

Jules laughed. 'People like your Webster have contacted

me before. The English are using me as a contact in case they need help.'

'But it is not going to help me find Stirling . . . ' Ian said despondently.

Jean had been scowling at the Englishman for the past few minutes. 'I'm not sure if I like the idea of being used by the English like this,' he protested, his blue eyes blazing. 'You shouldn't either, Jules! We are at war. They are our enemies and here we are, helping their spies!' he shouted angrily.

Jules calmly refilled Jean's glass. 'England is at war with the revolutionary tyranny, Jean, and so are we,' he reminded his impetuous friend. 'When the tyranny ends so will the war.'

Jean bit his lip and fell silent.

Ian looked utterly dejected. 'The likelihood of finding Stirling seems hopeless,' he admitted.

Jules strode over and gripped his shoulder resolutely. 'We will try!' he promised. 'You have a few days yet.'

Ian looked blank.

'Jean is leaving to search for the fourth member of your group,' Jules revealed. 'Susan's grandfather.'

Ian rose, his face alive with hope again. 'You know where he is?'

'No, but Jean will start at the farmhouse where you were arrested and follow the trail.'

'I will find him,' Jean vowed, draining his glass.

'Meanwhile, we shall search for your James Stirling,' Jules declared, patting Ian gently on the back.

Jean embraced Jules. 'You'll hear from me in three days at the latest,' he promised.

Jules kissed him on both cheeks. 'Take care, Jean.'

'Yes, good luck, Jean,' said Ian, shaking hands. 'And thank you.'

With a fearless wave Jean departed.

Jules poured more wine to help ease the tension. 'If anybody can find Susan's grandfather Jean can,' he said.

'And what about James Stirling?'

Jules sat down next to Ian. 'There *is* someone who springs to mind,' he said. 'Léon Colbert. We have shared many escapades. Léon moves in a wide circle and knows many people . . . Perhaps *he* is James Stirling!'

Ian drank to try and dull the pain in his head even more. 'Can you introduce us?' he asked earnestly.

'Very easily. Léon is coming here tomorrow, bringing a physician to examine Susan.'

Ian managed a smile of relief and hope. 'That's worth a toast!' he cried, clinking glasses with Jules.

Just then Barbara came in looking very tired and tense with worry. She went straight over to Ian. 'It's Susan . . . ' she murmured. 'She seems to be getting worse . . . '

8

Betrayal Everywhere

At dawn the Doctor rose in the still, quiet *Conciergerie*. He put
on his cloak and his fine plumed hat, picked up his stick and
his papers, and cautiously made his way along the narrow
passages to the vault. The early sun was streaming gloriously
through the cell windows and the air seemed much less
oppressive than it had the previous day. The Doctor slowed
as he reached the alcove. The besozzled gaoler was lying
across his table snoring like a rhinoceros. Satisfying himself
that the fellow was oblivious of his surroundings, the Doctor
started to run towards the steps leading to the courtyard. He
had almost reached them when somebody loomed out of the
shadows and barred his way.

'Good morning, Citizen Representative of Pontoise . . .'
boomed Lemaître's voice. 'I trust you slept well?'

The Doctor stopped in his tracks, his plumes quivering
with frustration. He smiled sourly at Lemaître. 'Thank you.
I did not!' he snapped. 'The bed was hard and the fleas . . .
Well, delicacy forbids . . .'

'I am so sorry,' Lemaître said humbly.

'I daresay you are. But if I catch the plague, apologies are
unlikely to have much effect,' retorted the Doctor.

Stirring, the gaoler dragged his head off the table and
stared woozily at them. Then he staggered to his feet and
gathered up the pile of dirty plates. 'I'd better feed the pigs
. . .' he grumbled, bowing to them and shuffling away.

'Poor pigs!' the Doctor muttered scornfully.

Lemaître took his arm. 'Come, Citizen, we'll have
breakfast,' he proposed pleasantly. 'You'll need something

inside you. I've an idea that today will be quite eventful . . . '

As the daylight pierced the cracks in the shutters, Ian Chesterton lay asleep on the sofa wrapped in a blanket. Jules Renan was sitting at the table studying maps and documents. Although he had not slept all night, he looked fresh and alert. All at once an urgent banging on the front door woke Ian with a start. Signalling to him to keep quiet, Jules drew his pistol and ran across to the window.

After a nerve-racking pause, Danielle tapped at the door and came in. 'A message from Léon: the physician refuses to come here,' she reported.

Ian sat up abruptly. 'But we've got to do something for Susan,' he insisted.

Jules nodded. 'Yes, we must take Susan to the physician.'

'I will arrange a carriage for them,' Danielle murmured, leaving the room.

Ian scrambled to his feet, wincing at the lingering pain in his head.

'You must remain here,' Jules informed him firmly. 'It will be less suspicious if the women go alone. Barbara can go with Susan. It is not far.'

Ian looked very unhappy with the plan. 'I don't like to lose sight of them so soon after finding them again, Jules,' he objected.

'Please, you must *trust* me,' Jules said. Besides, we have to arrange your meeting with Léon Colbert.'

Ian wandered restlessly around the room. 'When can I see him?'

Jules smiled. 'With luck, it will all be over today and you can all leave France together.'

Ian sighed helplessly and shrugged. 'All right, Jules. If you are sure it is safe . . . '

Jules patted his arm. 'I will go and fetch Susan and Barbara.'

Left alone, Ian started biting his nails nervously as he stared into the sunlit street. The return of daylight made him feel exposed. 'Let's hope we can trust the physician . . . .' he murmured.

* * *

An hour later Barbara and Susan arrived at the physician's scruffy little garret in Montmartre. By now the sun was well up and although all Paris was bathed in hot brightness, the garret was dark and damp. All kinds of barbaric surgical instruments were hanging around the mouldy walls and bottles of sludgy medicines filled the worm-eaten shelves. Susan sat on a stool gazing in dread at the bald little man with his cracked spectacles and his grubby apron as he walked round and round his patient rubbing his hands together. She was shivering and her skin looked like plaster.

'Yes, my dear, you appear to be suffering from a feverish chill. It's nothing very serious . . . ' the physician told her, in a voice like creaking hinges.

Barbara, who hovered anxiously nearby, murmured 'Thank goodness,' and instantly regretted her lapse into English.

The physician scowled at her and then peered more closely at Susan's chalky, perspiring face. 'I'm rather surprised by the young lady's condition,' he rasped. 'Any idea how you came to catch it?'

Susan shrugged miserably, flinching from his foul breath. 'I have done nothing unusual,' she replied, choosing her French words very carefully.

The smelly little man turned to Barbara. 'Has she been eating properly?' he inquired slyly.

Barbara forced a grin. 'She eats like a horse.'

Darting out talon-like fingers, the physician seized Susan's hands and turned them over. 'Your hands, my dear! They are badly blistered . . . ' he commented suspiciously.

'Yes, I know,' mumbled Susan. 'I've been . . . gardening a lot.'

Barbara hurriedly hid her own blistered hands behind her back. 'Can you help her please, Doctor?' she asked. 'We know you are busy and . . . '

'Yes, I can treat her,' grated the physician, rubbing his leathery hands together. 'It's a simple matter of blood-letting. Unfortunately I shall have to fetch some leeches . . . You have called rather early in the day.'

Susan turned to Barbara with a look of horror.

'I was intending to go out first thing for them anyway . . . '

the seedy little quack went on, smiling fawningly at them. 'You are welcome to wait here.'

Barbara went over and put her arm comfortingly around Susan. 'Perhaps it would be better if we called back later,' she suggested.

The physician scuttled to the door. 'No! You must wait here!' he croaked, as if afraid of something. 'By all means make yourselves at home . . . ' he scurried out and slammed the door hard.

Susan shuddered. 'I don't like him, Barbara, or the idea of having leeches stuck all over me,' she said weakly.

Barbara nodded. 'Anyway, I had the feeling he suspected us.' She helped Susan to her feet. 'Come on, Susan, let's get out of here.'

They waited a few minutes to give the physician time to leave the neighbourhood and then hurried to the door. Barbara turned the handle this way and that, but the door would not budge. They were caught once more, like animals in a trap.

They waited in the stifling, smelly garret for what seemed like hours and hours. There was nothing that looked safe to drink and only the slightest of fresh breezes blew in through the tiny window.

From time to time Barbara picked up the stool and tried to break down the stout wooden door, but it was useless. 'That door's even stronger than it looks . . . ' she gasped, collapsing onto the stool in despair after her umpteenth attempt at escape.

Suddenly they heard the stamping of boots up the narrow, winding stairs from the street. Barbara ran across to listen at the door, while Susan sat shivering in a threadbare armchair.

'If I'm wrong there won't be any repercussions, will there?' Barbara heard the physician's voice whining outside the door.

'Don't you worry, Citizen,' replied a hearty, gruff character. 'You'll probably pick up a nice little reward.'

Barbara backed away to comfort Susan as the door was unlocked and flung open. They found themselves staring at half a dozen muskets wielded by guards from the prison in their long narrow trousers, motley tunics and floppy nightcap hats.

'Like rabbits in a burrow!' leered the sergeant-in-command, striding in and grabbing his captives. 'Citizen Lemaître *will* be pleased.'

Ian Chesterton had been pacing round and round the dining table in feverish agitation, from time to time going to the window to peer into the glaringly sunlit street. But there was still no sign of Barbara and Susan, and he was beginning to fear that they would never see the Doctor again. Eventually he heard the front door open and close. Hurrying to investigate, he bumped into Jules in the doorway.

'Jules, Susan and Barbara have still not returned,' he said, his usually placid features creased with anxiety.

Jules waved his hands reassuringly. 'It is not unusual to be kept waiting at the physician's these days,' he replied.

Ian went back to the window, unconvinced. 'Something must have gone wrong, Jules,' he insisted.

Jules clasped his arm. 'They will be quite safe. Now, listen: I have arranged a meeting for you with Léon Colbert,' he said, smiling.

But Ian moved away again. 'Colbert can wait. I am more concerned about the two girls.'

Jules sighed and raised his arms in resignation. 'If it will make you feel any happier I will go and collect Barbara and Susan myself,' he offered. 'But if you really want to meet Colbert you will have to hurry. He moves around all the time. This may be your only chance.'

Ian thought for a moment. His head was still very tender and the heat was growing as oppressive as it had been the previous day. He was feeling pretty grim. 'Jules, you promise me you will go straight to the physician's?' he pleaded.

'I promise.'

Reluctantly Ian nodded his agreement.

'I explained some of your story to Léon,' Jules revealed. 'You must go alone. Léon is waiting at a disused church.'

Ian looked very disappointed. 'Then he is not James Stirling?'

'No,' said Jules, sitting down at the table and taking pen, ink and paper from the drawer. 'I will draw you a map. You must not waste any more time.'

Once again Susan and Barbara stood in the airless dank bowels of the *Conciergerie* flanked by their escort of soldiers, while the grinning gaoler swaggered up and down in front of them bursting with satisfaction.

'So, you thought you could escape!' he sneered, gloating at each in turn as he passed. 'We're not such nincompoops as you took us for, sweet ladies.'

At that moment, Lemaître's tall figure appeared from the dark passage leading to his room.

The gaoler strutted over to him. 'Two recaptured prisoners, Citizen!' he reported proudly.

Lemaître stared impassively at the two girls and then motioned the gaoler to withdraw with him out of earshot. As they talked, the gaoler kept glancing back at his two captives and nodding energetically.

'What do you think they're saying?' Susan whispered feebly, very weak after the hot march from Montmartre.

Before Barbara could reply, the gaoler came swaggering back to them and Lemaître looked on, an eerie figure in the shadows.

The jailer ordered two guards to take Susan back to the dungeon.

'Barbara!' Susan gasped, as she was seized and dragged away.

Barbara tried to follow, but the gaoler grabbed her arm with brutal ferocity. 'Not you, Mademoiselle,' he leered. 'You're wanted for questioning.'

It was torture for Barbara to listen to Susan's faint cries of desperation in the distance, while she herself was forced across the alcove to Lemaître. Lemaître waved his hand and she was propelled along the narrow dark passage and into his room at the end. She tried to struggle, but she was far too exhausted. In the bare room she was confronted by a tall cloaked figure standing with its back to her and staring out of the small barred window. With its tall plumed hat, the figure reminded her of the Spanish Inquisition.

Swallowing a cry of panic and despair, Barbara resolved to say nothing. She would betray nothing and nobody, whatever they did to her.

'Citizen Lemaître said you might like to interrogate this prisoner,' the gaoler growled.

The mysterious figure raised an arm and waved the ruffian away. As soon as the door had slammed shut behind the gaoler, the tall figure slowly turned to face the prisoner.

Barbara's eyes almost popped out. She uttered a strangled gasp of disbelief and delight. 'Doctor!' she breathed. '*Doctor!*'

The beaming Time Lord came forward and clasped her hands. 'Barbara . . . Barbara, you're safe!' he murmured, hugging her tightly and laughing with quiet but heartfelt relief.

His heart pounding and his nerves tingling, Ian crept cautiously down the worn steps into the rubble-strewn crypt of the abandoned church. Short stubby pillars supported arches behind which deep unfathomable shadows stretched on either side. Straw, nettles, glass, bricks and tiles were scattered everywhere and it was dark as a cave, except for odd shafts of sun streaming through holes in the church floor above.

Suddenly he heard a movement behind him. He whipped round and was just able to distinguish a tall cloaked figure in the shadows. 'Léon . . . ?' he whispered tentatively.

'You must be Ian,' answered the ghostly shape.

'Yes, I am.'

'Are you alone?' Colbert inquired casually in his resonant voice.

Ian confirmed that he was. 'Jules Renan said that you might be able to help us, Léon.'

'Us?'

'Myself and my friends,' Ian explained, breaking off as he heard faint sounds from the shadowy archways. Gesturing to Colbert to keep quiet, Ian slowly turned round.

He found himself confronting two militiamen with their bayonets and musket trained on his heart.

'Soldiers!' he gasped, turning back to Colbert.

The Frenchman was covering him with a pair of ornate cocked pistols. 'Poor Englishman. So crude and lacking in finesse,' Léon laughed. 'You walked right into our trap, did you not, Ian!'

Ian glanced back at the soldiers and then at the murky steps behind Léon. 'Forget about escape,' Colbert scoffed contemptuously. 'And as for being rescued? Nobody will come here, take my word.'

Ian squinted into the gloom, trying to form a clearer impression of who he was up against. 'If I do not return, Jules will investigate,' he challenged.

Colbert came forward into a shaft of light. 'By that time we shall have taken care of him too,' he retorted. He signalled to the soldiers.

They grabbed Ian and dragged him against a pillar with iron rings set into it. His wrists were firmly shackled to the rings with stout chains.

'Well, you never know who your friends are . . . ' Ian remarked with a sour smile.

Léon walked nonchalantly over to him. 'Our association would have had to end anyway,' he revealed. 'Jules already suspects that a . . . a traitor, if you want to use that word . . . is working inside our organisation. We were about to close in on him too.'

'But what on earth do you want from me?' Ian demanded.

Léon smiled. 'Information of course.'

Ian smiled too, as if any suggestion that he would talk was beneath his contempt.

Léon frowned. 'Oh, you *will* co-operate . . . eventually,' he said drily. He smiled again. 'Think about it, Ian. We have plenty of time.' Léon turned and walked away into the shadows.

'He's giving you time to consider,' hissed one of the soldiers.

Ian struggled half-heartedly against the tight iron shackles. 'I do not need any time,' he retorted defiantly. 'I know nothing of any value.'

The soldier slashed his bayonet to and fro in Ian's face. 'We'll decide that when you talk,' he sneered, hitting Ian in the stomach with the butt of his musket. 'And you'll talk,' he promised, hitting Ian again so that he doubled over in agony. 'Oh yes, you'll certainly talk . . . '

Lemaître's noble features creased in a slow and thoughtful smile as he listened through the door to the excited conversation in English between the old man and the young woman taking place in the interrogation room. As far as he could make out, his suspicions were proving correct.

'Doctor, we began to think we'd never see you again . . . ' Barbara was saying, overjoyed to be reunited at last.

The Doctor chuckled wryly. 'You should have discovered by now, my dear, that you can't get rid of the old Doctor as easily as that,' he chided her. Then he suddenly grew very serious. 'But what about Susan? Do you know where she is?'

'She's here in the *Conciergerie*, Doctor. She was arrested with me,' Barbara told him, breathless with surprise.

The Doctor's eyebrows shot up. 'Susan's here?' he exclaimed. 'Is she all right?'

'Fine, except that she caught a bit of a chill. She's in the dungeon.'

The Doctor frowned. 'Then we must find Chesterton and get everyone back to the TARDIS at once,' he declared decisively.

'Doctor, we know where Ian is,' said Barbara, sinking into one of the chairs. 'We were all hiding at a house owned by Jules Renan . . . '

'Splendid . . . ' muttered the Doctor, pacing thoughtfully up and down in his finery. 'Then all we need now is a plan of escape. Where is this house?'

Before Lemaître could hear Barbara's reply, the gaoler came waddling breathlessly along the passage.

'Not now, gaoler, I'll speak to you later,' Lemaître snapped, a frown like a thundercloud settling on his brow.

But the gaoler was determined to speak. 'I've just received a message for you from the First Deputy . . . ' he mumbled, nodding significantly at the two soldiers flanking the door.

'Well?' Lemaître demanded, reluctantly moving out of earshot.

'Citizen Robespierre wants to see you immediately,' the

gaoler confided. 'He said it was of the greatest importance.'

Lemaître banged his fists together in frustration. He dearly wished to eavesdrop on the conversation in the room, but he equally appreciated the folly of delaying after a summons from Robespierre himself.

'The First Deputy did say immediately . . . ' the gaoler repeated with a knowing grin.

'Yes, yes, yes . . . ' Lemaître nodded tetchily. 'Listen, gaoler, has the young girl been locked away?'

'I saw to it myself, Citizen. Just as you ordered.'

Lemaître leaned forward, thrusting his face into the ruffian's. 'She is to remain in her cell whatever happens,' he instructed grimly. 'You understand? Under no circumstances is her door to be opened.'

The gaoler nodded obsequiously. 'As you say, Citizen. Under no circum . . . '

'And if my order if disobeyed I'll have you guillotined . . . '

The gaoler stared mesmerised at Lemaître's brilliant white teeth only millimetres from his bulbous nose and nodded frantically. Then Lemaître beckoned to the two sentries to follow him and strode rapidly away. Gulping and quaking in his boots, the gaoler watched them go and then scurried back to the alcove on his stumpy little legs.

At that moment, on the other side of the door, the Doctor was snapping his fingers and beaming with inspiration. 'That's it, I've got it!' he cried.

Barbara seemed not to hear him. She was still mulling over the mistakes she had made. 'I was a fool even to think of taking Susan to the physician. It's my fault entirely,' she confessed gloomily.

'As it happens things have worked out quite well,' the Doctor contradicted her. 'It might have taken ages for us all to find one another otherwise.'

Barbara looked suddenly hopeful. 'Do you really think we have any chance of getting out of here?' she asked.

'I most certainly do,' the Doctor nodded vehemently. 'My voice appears to carry some weight around here.'

Barbara grinned. 'I'm not surprised in that get-up,' she said, pointing at the Doctor's elaborate costume.

The Doctor fixed her with a stern look. 'Now, pay

attention, Barbara. I'm going outside now. You must wait a few minutes. Then you must walk out of the room and out of the *Conciergerie*.'

Barbara gaped at the white-haired Time Lord as if he had just gone mad. 'Are you *serious*?' she eventually exclaimed.

The Doctor grasped her shoulders and stared earnestly into her eyes. 'Of course I am, Barbara. There's no time to explain. Don't ask questions, just do as I say.'

'But what about Susan? Surely you haven't forgotten about her?'

'*I'll* take care of Susan,' the Doctor insisted adamantly. 'We shall be along, don't you worry. We'll meet at the house.'

Barbara looked very doubtful about the whole idea. 'But Doctor, what if . . . '

The Doctor waved his stick and shook his head so that his tall white plumes waved majestically in the shafts of sunlight streaming through the window into the poky room. 'Now do stop arguing, Barbara. You know perfectly well that my schemes always work,' he declared, gazing down his nose at the mere mortal.

Barbara watched helplessly as he opened the door and peered cautiously outside to check that the coast was clear.

'Just wait a few minutes and then leave . . . ' he reminded her. Seconds later he was gone.

Against her better judgement, Barbara found herself nodding at empty space. A thousand questions that she should have asked and that the Doctor should have answered flooded into her mind. But it was too late now.

The Doctor strode authoritatively into the alcove and rapped on the table with his stick. 'Where is Lemaître?' he demanded loftily.

The gaoler hurriedly corked his cognac bottle and wiped his blubbery lips. 'The Citizen has gone to see First Deputy Robespierre.'

The Doctor concealed his secret smile of relief beneath a scowl of irritation. 'Dear, dear, dear. I wanted to see him most urgently,' he complained, beginning to pace restlessly around the table. 'You see, I have interrogated the young woman and I am convinced that she is a dangerous member of the anti-revolutionary party . . . '

The gaoler's eyes widened expectantly.

'I'm sure she could reveal the names of all the leading traitors in France . . . ' the Doctor added, tapping his nose with the handle of his walking stick in imitation of Lemaître.

'Perhaps we could make her talk,' the gaoler suggested eagerly.

The Doctor continued his pacing as though deep in thought. 'No. No chance, my friend. She would die before she betrayed her treacherous associates,' he declared. He sat on the edge of the table, frowning with exaggerated concentration. 'Oh, if only there was some way we could make use of her . . . Some way we could use her to lead us to her brothers and sisters . . . '

The gaoler knitted his apelike brows in the effort to come up with a suggestion. He did not notice the Doctor's impatient sidelong glances in his direction, willing him to have a brainwave.

There was a long chasm-like pause.

'Perhaps we could . . . ' the gaoler began.

'Yes? Yes, what is it?' cried the Doctor, jumping up from the table.

The gaoler concentrated extremely hard. 'Well, Citizen, if the young lady was allowed to sort of escape she could be followed . . . I mean, she'd go and meet the traitors and we'd follow her and arrest them all . . . ' The gaoler sank back on his chair and wiped his brow as if the idea had taken a lot out of him.

The Doctor gazed at the gaoler in breathless admiration. 'My dear fellow!' he exclaimed after a suitable pause. 'My dear fellow, what a *superb* idea! Why didn't I think of it myself?'

The gaoler beamed modestly and shrugged.

'That is exactly what we shall do,' the Doctor continued enthusiastically. 'Lemaître will be absolutely delighted with you.' The Doctor walked round the table and spoke confidentially into the flattered ruffian's cauliflower ear. 'Open the prison gates, gaoler, and then keep your men out of sight. Sooner or later the girl will find her way out and we shall simply follow her!'

The gaoler looked ecstatic. Nodding with conspiratorial eagerness, he scuttled away to do the Doctor's bidding.

The Doctor smiled smugly to himself and then turned and hurried away along the vault towards the dungeon.

After a while Barbara peeped out of Lemaître's room and then ran along the narrow passage to the alcove. The prison looked deserted. She ran along the vault and up the steps to the courtyard. Reaching the open air, she sighed with relief. The Doctor appeared to have arranged everything perfectly. Taking a deep breath, she plucked up her courage and walked towards the main gateway, hoping against hope that nothing would go wrong now.

9

Illusions Shattered

In the secluded secrecy of the ruined crypt, Ian hung from
the iron shackles. His wrists were bleeding and his whole
body was racked with pain because of the awkward posture
he was being forced into – almost on tiptoe with most of his
weight suspended from his wrists. The two soldiers were
sitting some distance away, swigging rough red wine and
munching crusty loaves. Ian groaned in agony, his parched
throat burning and his tongue rasping against the dry roof of
his mouth like sandpaper.

One of the bored soldiers got up and slouched over.
'Getting impatient, are we?' he sneered. 'That's a good
sign. Citizen Colbert really knows how to make pigs like you
talk. Leave them alone. Let them suffer and have time to
think . . . Now me, I'd use more instant methods . . . ' The
young bully raised his musket butt aloft ready to bring it
down in a savage swipe across Ian's face.

Stop that!'

Léon Colbert emerged from the arches and strode up,
shoving the sadistic militiaman aside. He smiled apologetically at Ian. 'I fear my men are rather impatient,' he
admitted quietly. 'I really do not want you to come to any
harm, Chesterton, but I know that you possess information
that is vital to the cause I believe in.'

Ian did his best to smile back despite the pain. 'You are
wasting your time with me, Colbert. I am very small fry,' he
retorted.

Léon folded his arms and shook his head wearily. 'You
really cannot expect me to believe that,' he protested. 'We

learned about the existence of James Stirling two months ago. We have been searching for him ever since.'

Ian gritted his teeth. 'We?' he echoed.

Colbert's face became almost friendly. 'I have been loyal to the Revolution from the very beginning,' he explained. 'If you had known France six years ago – before the *Bastille* – I think you would understand.'

Ian managed a pale smile. The irony of his situation was almost comical. 'Oh, I do understand, Léon, believe me,' he replied. 'But I cannot help you.'

'Or you *will* not help us.' Léon stared into the sunlight pouring from a hole in the roof. 'France will never be anything until we have purged her of these high-born leeches who have sucked her life-blood for so many centuries . . . ' he burst out passionately.

Ian tried to ease the terrible strain on his chafed and bloody wrists. 'I understand your mission, Léon,' he repeated, 'but you must believe that I cannot help you.'

Colbert looked genuinely upset. 'Ian, you can save yourself so much suffering if you talk. This is your only chance.'

Colbert paused, waiting for Ian to respond to his appeal. Ian stared back at him, mute and defiant.

'You realise that when I have finished with you you will be guillotined?' Colbert continued in desperation. 'But if you co-operate then I have the power to free you.' Again Colbert paused.

Ian tried to laugh and was racked with a choking coughing fit. 'This is absurd . . . ' he gasped when he recovered. 'Jules must have told you all I know.'

Colbert drew closer to his victim. 'Ah yes, what did Jules say?' he mocked. 'That Webster asked you to deliver a vital message to James Stirling.'

Ian nodded readily. 'Quite right. I do not know Stirling's identity. If I did, I obviously would not have come here.'

Colbert smiled sardonically. 'But you *are* here, Ian,' he said menacingly. 'You must know about their organisation. Webster would never have trusted you otherwise.' He thrust his face into Ian's, his eyes hardening. 'Now, who sent you from England? How did you get to France? Who are your other contacts here? Be sensible, save yourself from the guillotine . . . '

Ian shook his head helplessly. 'You would never believe my story,' he moaned, growing weaker.

'Let me be the judge of that! How did you get to France?'

Ian licked his cracking lips and struggled to take a deep breath against the pull of the shackles. 'I flew here . . . in a wooden box . . . with three friends . . . '

Colbert's face remained impassive, but his fists clenched around the pistols in his belt.

'When I left England it was the year 1963 . . . ' Ian continued recklessly, dissolving into a choking laugh at the comical sound of his explanation in French.

With a savage oath Colbert stepped back and signalled to one of the soldiers. Gripping his musket with the fixed bayonet held firmly in front of him, the soldier marched inexorably towards the helpless captive hanging against the pillar in chains. Ian struggled pathetically for a few seconds and then steeled himself for the dreaded slash of steel.

Just before the soldier reached him, a shadowy figure suddenly emerged into a shaft of sunlight at the far end of the crypt.

'That's enough, Léon. Let him go!'

The soldier froze. Ian's half-closed eyes snapped open to see Jules Renan advancing cautiously towards him behind Léon Colbert, with a pistol covering his captors. Next moment, the other soldier sitting by himself levelled his musket at Jules. But before he could shoot, Jules swung sideways and fired at his head. Léon's hands flew to his pistols, but Jules hurled his discharged weapon into his face with deadly accuracy. Léon shrieked and fell backwards with blood spurting from a deep gash between his eyes. Meanwhile the soldier nearest Ian had managed to cock his musket and swing round to aim at Jules.

Summoning the last vestiges of his strength, Ian threw all his weight onto his lacerated wrists, lifted his feet high in the air and swung his legs in a scything arc. He hit the soldier on the side of the head and knocked him sideways. As he fell, the soldier fired his musket and the ball zipped past Ian's head, missing him by millimetres. Ian caught sight of Léon scrambling to his feet and drawing his weapons.

117

'Jules! Look out!' he yelled.

Jules grabbed the toppling soldier and spun round using him as a shield. Colbert fired both pistols simultaneously. The soldier's body jerked horribly and Jules let him slump to the ground.

'*Traitor*!' Jules gasped, gaping incredulously at Léon. 'So it is *you* who has been betraying our cause . . . '

Colbert stared contemptuously back at him. 'Traitor?' he mocked. 'Not I, Jules. The traitors are you and your cronies who work against the government of the People . . . ' Colbert had noticed the undischarged musket lying beside the soldier that Jules had killed, and he was slowly backing towards it keeping his eyes on Jules.

Jules reached unobtrusively into his coat pocket and drew out a second pistol. As Colbert turned and dived for the musket there was a flash and a bang from Jules's hand. Colbert sank to his knees with a look of surprise on his bloody face. For several seconds he knelt in front of Jules like a priest in front of an altar. Then he toppled forward onto his face in the rubble and weeds.

Jules hurried across to release Ian from his iron bonds. 'We must move quickly . . . ' he muttered, using the pistol barrel to lever open the links of the chains.

Ian was almost crying with relief. 'I thought I was dreaming or going mad when you appeared . . . ' he stuttered, sick with shock. 'What made you come here?'

'Bad news, Ian. Your fears were justified. Barbara and Susan have been arrested at the physician's. I came for you at once.'

Ian looked utterly distraught. 'We must get after them immediately!' he cried, tugging at the chains with renewed vigour.

Jules shook his head as he eased Ian's bruised hands out of the forced shackles. 'No. First we must return to the house.'

'But the soldiers will probably be waiting for us,' Ian objected.

Jules tore his clean handkerchief in two and helped Ian wrap a couple of makeshift bandages round his wrists. 'I think not,' he said. 'I feel sure that Léon would have relished the satisfaction of arresting me himself. Anyway, we shall have to risk it,' he insisted.

Jules led the way back to the house through the side streets constantly making detours and doubling back to confuse anyone who might be tailing them. As far as possible they avoided the small bands of militiamen and *sans-culottes* which roamed the city taking the law into their own hands on the slightest suspicion.

'I wish I knew what has happened to the Doctor,' Ian muttered as Jules helped him along a dark alleyway. 'He would know what we ought to do for best . . .'

Susan lay on the lumpy iron bed in the dungeon staring at the mould on the glistening ceiling and listening to the hypnotic drip-drip of the water and the intermittent squeaking and scuttling of the invisible rats. She felt a little better physically and even her blisters had stopped hurting, but her spirit was utterly broken, and she felt that there was now no hope at all for herself or her friends. Soon she expected to find herself back in the dreaded blood-coloured tumbril with Barbara and Ian, rumbling through the jeering crowds to the guillotine. As for her grandfather, she doubted whether he was even alive any longer.

Suddenly she caught sight of an eye blinking at her behind the spy-hole in the dungeon door. Her stomach heaved with revulsion as she imagined the slimy, squat little gaoler ogling her in her misery. 'What is it? What do you want?' she mumbled wearily, levering herself up onto her elbows.

'Susan . . . Susan can you hear me?' whispered a familiar voice.

She felt a thrill of joy shoot through her exhausted body. For a few seconds she feared that she might have become delirious with fever, especially when the eye at the spy-hole suddenly winked roguishly at her. 'Grandfather . . . ?' she murmured, scrambling to her feet and running to the door. 'Grandfather, is it really you? What happened to you? How did you escape from the farmhouse?' she blurted out, her words tripping over one another in her excitement.

'I can't explain all that now, child, there isn't time,' replied the Doctor in an undertone, putting his mouth to the spy-hole. 'I've got to work fast.'

'Barbara's here somewhere . . . ' Susan whispered, trying to control herself.

'Yes, yes, I've already taken care of her. She should be well away by now,' the Doctor interrupted urgently. 'Now, listen, my dear, I have to go away for a little while. But I'll be back, never fear. And then I'll get us both safely out of here.'

Susan stood up on tiptoe to see more clearly through the spy-hole and make sure she was not dreaming or imagining things. 'Do be careful, Grandfather,' she pleaded, tears of relief welling in her eyes.

'Yes, yes, child. Now don't fuss and don't worry . . . '

The mouth abruptly vanished from the spy-hole and Susan heard the Doctor's footsteps receding on the flag-stones. Trembling with anticipation, she lay on the bed again and tried to remain calm, scarcely daring to breath for fear of somehow giving her grandfather away.

The Doctor bumped into the gaoler by the alcove.

The gaoler looked at him thunderstruck. 'Citizen! I thought you . . . Didn't you take some guards and follow the released prisoner?' he squawked, his eyes bulging.

The Doctor stared down his nose at the quaking ruffian. 'Certainly not!' he retorted icily. 'I naturally assumed that *you* were going to follow her.' He shook his plumes imperiously. 'I am hardly suitably attired to go chasing after escaping prisoners, am I?'

The gaoler clutched his tousled, bandaged head in disbelief. 'But, Citizen, I can't leave the prison . . . ' he whimpered.

The Doctor clicked his tongue sternly. 'Well, well, and what do you suppose Citizen Lemaître is going to say?' he snapped. 'He's bound to want to know whose idea it was.'

The gaoler sank into his chair, his blotchy face a mask of sheer misery. 'It was my idea,' he mumbled. 'Citizen, you must help me . . . Please help me . . . '

The Doctor frowned gravely. 'I'll do my best,' he promised generously. 'Now, the way I see things . . . The young girl in the dungeon is also tied up in this business. We'll let her go and I *personally* will follow her and arrest the lot of them.' The Doctor shot out his hand. 'All I require from you is the key to the dungeon.'

But the gaoler looked aghast and gripped the key ring tightly in his podgy fists. 'Citizen Lemaître was very clear in his instructions,' he protested. 'Before he left he told me that if that door is opened, I will lose my head,.

The Doctor waved his arms contemptuously. 'Lemaître . . . Lemaître . . . Good heavens, man, can't you ever work on your own initiative?' he scoffed. 'I order you to open the child's cell immediately!'

But the gaoler shook his head adamantly. 'To lose one prisoner is bad enough,' he mumbled. 'To lose two would be the end of me. Citizen Lemaître will be back soon. You'll have to ask him. Until he says otherwise, that door remains locked.'

The Doctor was almost purple with outrage, but he realised that argument was futile. With a snort of exasperation he stalked off muttering darkly to himself.

Maximilien Marie Robespierre looked thinner and more drawn than ever as he paced ceaselessly to and fro in his tall, gloomy study hands twisted nervously in a knot behind his back. From time to time he paused to gaze down through the long windows into the courtyard below thronged with deputies and deputations, visiting provincial officials, representatives of the militant and cantankerous Paris Commune and all manner of petitioners, plotters and complainants.

All at once the double doors were flung open and Lemaître was shown in by a soldier. Robespierre rushed forward to greet him. 'At last, Lemaître!' he cried thankfully. He waved the soldier away with orders that he and his visitor must not be disturbed under any circumstances. Then he ushered Lemaître into a chair and resumed his restless, haunted pacing. 'The news is extremely serious, Citizen,' he confided. 'We have very little time.'

Lemaître looked up earnestly. 'I am completely at your service Citizen First Deputy,' he pledged. 'You have only to give the word.'

Robespierre bowed in acknowledgement. 'The Convention meets tomorrow,' he continued quietly. 'I have

121

discovered that certain influential members – traitors all of them – are planning to bring an indictment against a senior member . . . '

Lemaître rose gravely to his feet. 'You have their names?'

Robespierre seemed unaware of the question. He paced more relentlessly than ever. 'I realise that they are forever plotting, but this latest intelligence suggests that more and more of the Paris Commune are taking sides against me.' Robespierre stopped in front of his visitor, his greenish eyes blazing like emeralds. 'They plan to prevent me from speaking. They are determined to destroy me!'

Lemaître shook his head loyally. 'All is not yet lost. You still have many friends in the Convention,' he declared.

The First Deputy resumed his pacing again. 'But can I trust them? They may turn against me to save their own necks,' he speculated, his feeble voice sounding more transparent than ever as he waved his long bony fingers in an attempt to reinforce his argument. 'Mark my words, Lemaître, if their plot succeeds, tomorrow, the Twenty-Seventh of July, 1794 . . . the *Ninth Thermidor* . . . will be remembered in history as a momentous day.'

Lemaître's eyes shone with intense purpose. 'Give me the names of the rebels, Citizen! They will be executed at once!' he promised.

Robespierre paused, fixing Lemaître with his reptilian stare. 'Patience, Citizen,' he cautioned. 'They are not working in isolation. They know they will need the support of the military. Meetings must have been arranged . . . '

'By whom? Barras?'

'Paul Barras,' Robespierre nodded. 'It is my guess that he is the ringleader. But we must be absolutely certain before we strike. We shall not enjoy a second opportunity, Lemaître.'

The visitor tapped himself on the chin with the silver knob of his long cane. 'Tell me what I must do,' he murmured eagerly.

Robespierre moved closer and spoke very quietly as if he suspected that the very walls had ears. 'I understand Barras intends to leave Paris tonight, presumably for a meeting. I want to know where, with whom and the substance of the discussions. Armed with this information I may be able to defeat the enemies of the Revolution.'

Lemaître thought carefully. 'Barras might just be a decoy,' he warned.

Robespierre nodded grimly. 'Precisely my fear. By tonight my people will be everywhere . . . ' He drew even closer to Lemaître. 'But Barras is your *personal* responsibility.'

Lemaître bowed. 'I am honoured. I shall not fail,' he vowed, moving to the door. With his fingers on the handle he paused and turned. 'Against which member will the indictment be brought?' he asked.

There was a long silence.

'Against Robespierre,' came the ice-cold reply. 'Against me . . . Against the Revolution itself . . . '

Ian and Jules approached the house very cautiously, but there was no sign of Léon Colbert's associates. Jules's gamble appeared to have paid off.

'We shall have to give up the house soon,' Jules told Ian as they entered the dining room. 'It is becoming too dangerous now.'

They both stopped in their tracks. There, dozing in an armchair, sat Barbara.

'Barbara, we thought you'd been arrested again!' cried Ian joyfully.

Barbara opened her eyes and smiled. 'Yes, we were, but when we reached the *Conciergerie* we met the Doctor!'

Ian's face brightened even more. 'The Doctor? At the prison?'

'Yes; dressed up as if he was running the Revolution single-handed. From the look of things, he's got half the people there taking orders right, left and centre,' Barbara chuckled.

'That sounds like the Doctor all right!' Ian laughed, feeling better already. He glanced around the room. 'But what about Susan? Isn't she with you?'

Barbara quickly explained what had happened at the prison.

Ian whistled in astonishment at the Time Lord's bare-faced audacity. 'Just walked out did you . . . ? I don't know how he gets away with it half the time!' he exclaimed. 'What did the Doctor tell you?'

Barbara tried hard to remember. 'Nothing very much. We hardly had any chance to talk. But he should be here with Susan soon. No doubt we'll hear all about his adventures then.'

'Several times over,' Ian said wryly.

Jules looked utterly bewildered as he tried to follow their conversation in English. 'Please . . . the Doctor?' he inquired.

'Susan's grandfather,' Barbara explained, reverting to French. Suddenly she noticed Ian's bandaged forearms. 'Ian, whatever happened to your wrists?' she asked in a shocked tone.

Ian shrugged. 'Let's just say they fell into the wrong hands,' he quipped bravely. 'Fortunately Jules arrived in the nick of time.' He took Barbara's hands and frowned. 'You look as if you've been digging roads!' he commented wryly.

Barbara quickly explained. Then she asked where Léon had got to. There was a hollow, awkward silence.

'Léon is dead. I killed him,' Jules eventually replied in a hushed voice.

Barbara looked horrified. 'You *killed* him?' she exclaimed, jumping up.

Jules raised his arms helplessly. 'Barbara, I fear that Léon was the traitor we were looking for,' he said bleakly. 'He deserved to die. There was no choice.'

Ian put his arm round Barbara's shoulders. 'It was the only way, Barbara,' he assured her.

Barbara backed away from the two men, staring at them as if they were insane. 'What on earth do you mean, a traitor?' she protested incredulously, sinking onto a chair.

'As soon as I got to the church Léon turned on me,' Ian told her. 'He was prepared to murder me in cold blood.'

'Léon was betraying us and our movement,' Jules explained sadly.

Barbara tossed her head defiantly. 'He was only a traitor in *your* eyes, Jules!' she retorted aggressively. 'To his own people he was a patriot.'

124

Ian sat down beside her. 'Barbara, please try to understand,' he pleaded. 'We have taken sides just by being here. It was Jules who shot Léon, but it could just as easily have been me who pulled the trigger . . . ' He held up his lacerated wrists. 'If Léon's soldiers had not already strung me up like a pig in an abattoir.'

Jules was staring resentfully at Barbara. 'I suppose Robespierre is a knight in shining armour in your eyes,' he said harshly.

Barbara jumped up again, bursting with indignation. 'Jules, just because an extremist like Robespierre behaves . . . '

Ian intervened again, drawing her aside. 'Barbara, Jules has saved my life. He and Jean saved all our lives. Their enemies are our enemies,' he argued earnestly.

There was a tense silence.

Eventually Barbara sat down again. 'Yes I know,' she conceded in a more subdued tone. 'But the Revolution is not all bad, Ian. Neither are the people who believed in it. It changed things for the whole world and good, honest people sacrificed their lives for that change . . . '

Ian shook his head irritably. 'Really, Barbara, we're not in your classroom at Coal Hill School now . . . ' he objected.

With a sigh of exasperation, Barbara stood up again and wandered away in defiant isolation. 'Take a look at your history books before you start making judgements . . . ' she challenged.

Jules had been struggling to follow the latter part of the dispute in English. History books . . . ?' he echoed, utterly perplexed. 'Whatever do you mean? There has never been a revolution like this before. Never in all history!'

Ian had become so worked up that it was all he could do to resist the temptation to reveal to Jules what the future held for France over the next one and a half centuries. But a sharp warning glance from Barbara reminded him of the Doctor's strict views about such things and so he reluctantly clammed up. But it was immensely frustrating to be able to see into the future and yet not be able to do anything to change it!

10

A Hard Bargain

The Doctor seemed to have been gone for hours. Susan lay in the foetid dungeon anxiously listening for some hint of his promised return. At long last she heard a movement outside the door.

'Grandfather, is that you? I thought you were never coming back,' she whispered, running to the door.

'Listen carefully,' the Doctor hissed through the spy-hole. 'I want you to crouch down on the floor behind the door and stay out of sight whatever happens, do you understand?'

Susan wanted to ask a dozen questions. 'But, Grandfather . . . '

'Do it now, child!' the Doctor commanded sternly. 'And don't move or make a sound.'

Trembling with fever and with nerves, Susan obeyed. Biting her fist to stop herself from crying out, she crouched against the wall and waited to see what would happen next, her heart pounding like mad.

The Doctor strode back to the alcove and found the gaoler slumped morosely over his table drinking cognac from yet another bottle.

'Where is Lemaître?' the Doctor demanded, banging the table with his stick. 'It's scandalous that I am kept waiting like this!'

'I'm expecting him back any time now,' mumbled the gaoler, scratching his bandaged head with the neck of the bottle. 'I don't know what he's going to say about all this business . . .'

'Neither do I!' the Doctor retorted sharply. 'The young girl has vanished!'

The gaoler gaped at the Doctor in total disbelief. Then he sprang up, dropping the bottle and snatching at his keys. 'Vanished?' he shrieked. He scuttled off along the vault feverishly searching for the dungeon key on the crowded ring. 'She can't be . . .'

Picking up the cognac bottle, the Doctor set off in pursuit. He found the mortified gaoler peering through the spy-hole and fumbling clumsily with the lock.

'She's gone . . . She's gone . . .' the gaoler repeated in a raucous croak, like a shocked parrot.

As he finally turned the key, the Doctor crept stealthily up behind him and hit him smartly over the head with the cognac bottle. The gaoler grunted and slid onto his knees against the doorframe, knocked almost senseless.

The Doctor pushed open the door and grabbed Susan's hand. 'Quickly, Susan, quickly!' he cried, dragging her out of the dungeon.

He was about to lock the gaoler in the cell when Lemaître's voice suddenly rang out like a death knell. 'Guards! Guards! Here at once!'

There was a confusion of shouts and running feet and several soldiers burst round the corner and surrounded them with levelled bayonets. Next moment, Lemaître himself appeared, smiling grimly.

The dazed gaoler staggered to his feet holding his freshly-wounded head. 'He tricked me, Citizen . . . He tricked me . . .' he complained pathetically, pointing at the Doctor.

Lemaître ignored him. 'Lock her away!' he ordered, poking Susan with his cane.

The guards bundled the tearful and terrified girl back into the dungeon and locked the door. Susan threw herself onto the bed and sobbed with bitter disappointment.

Lemaître thrust the fawning gaoler aside and confronted the Doctor with a cold but respectful expression. 'I think that it is time we had a little talk,' he proposed quietly, moving aside to let the Doctor precede him flanked by two guards.

The Doctor nodded vigorously and set off between his escorts in the direction of Lemaître's room. 'I couldn't agree more, Citizen,' he replied with an enigmatic smile.

As he strode into the austere interrogation room at the end of the narrow passage, the Doctor rapped indignantly on the flagstones with his walking stick. 'To start with I really must insist on that young girl's release,' he announced.

Lemaître shut the door behind him. 'Do you recognise this, Citizen?' he asked, holding up a small shiny object between his thumb and forefinger.

The Doctor squinted at the ring he had given to the tailor in part exchange for his new clothes and a shadow of doubt passed over his severe countenance. He quickly suppressed his fear as to how much Lemaître knew about him and shrugged absently. 'No, should I?' he replied, casually turning it over in his fingers.

Lemaître shot him a look which advised him not to play silly games. 'It is *your* ring, Citizen. You gave it in exchange for your splendid attire and your insignia of Provincial Deputy.'

The Doctor snorted with derision. 'I've never heard such an absurd fairy tale in all my life,' he protested.

Lemaître circled the outraged Time Lord. 'You appreciate that I could have had you arrested at any moment?' he remarked ominously.

The Doctor pondered this puzzling factor. 'Yes indeed. Why didn't you?' he inquired, offering the ring back to Lemaître.

'Please keep your ring, Citizen,' Lemaître requested, continuing to circle the Doctor with slow deliberation. 'I did not arrest you because, the political situation being as it is and my own situation being what it is, I need friends – even if they are enemies – people on whom I can call for help.' Lemaître stopped in front of his puzzled prisoner. 'And if I have some hold over them, then so much the better . . . '

There was a pause. The Doctor smiled wryly. 'No wonder you didn't want me to leave the prison.'

Lemaître smiled bleakly. 'I knew that I should never see you again if I let you leave.'

The Doctor tapped his nose with his stick. 'But you

relaxed things today. I could have walked out of the *Conciergerie* at any time . . . '

Lemaître waved his finger as if scolding a naughty child. 'And deserted your granddaughter? I think not.'

The Doctor threw back his head and regarded Lemaître with keen and searching curiosity.

Lemaître shrugged. 'I knew that so long as she was here you too would remain, even though your other two friends might have escaped . . . what were their names . . . Barbara and Ian?'

The Doctor stared down his nose. 'So, you knew all about us all the time?'

Lemaître tapped his ear with his cane. 'Listening at key-holes can be very informative,' he remarked with a grimace of distaste.

There was another pause while the two sized each other up like a pair of duellists.

'What is it you require from me?' the Doctor demanded at last.

Lemaître moved closer and lowered his voice confidentially. 'You and your friends obviously work with Jules Renan. I want to know where he operates from.'

'I've never met this man Jules Renan,' the Doctor retorted. 'I appreciate how much you want to find him and his associates, but if you are expecting me to betray him then you are a very poor judge of character, sir.'

Lemaître stepped even closer so that his nose was almost touching the Doctor's. 'If you wish your granddaughter to be released alive, then you will take me to Renan's hide-out,' he said menacingly.

The Doctor stepped back, shaking his head vehemently. 'I refuse. Never!' he shouted. 'I warn you, Citizen. You cannot blackmail me!'

As the sultry July heat beat down upon Paris, the tension had become almost tangible behind the half-closed shutters of Jules Renan's house. Barbara and Ian had tended one another's wounds and now they sat listening to the elegant mantel-clock relentlessly ticking away the minutes as they waited for Jules to return from his reconnoitre along the street in search of the Doctor and Susan.

'How much longer can we wait?' Ian eventually blurted out, breaking the oppressive silence between them.

Barbara wiped her glistening brow. 'Every time somebody walks past the house I think it's going to be them at last,' she laughed nervously.

Ian fidgeted awkwardly. 'I'm really sorry about Léon,' he said after another silence, 'but there was no other way. You must try to believe me, Barbara.'

She nodded glumly. 'I'm just so sick and tired of death, Ian. But we don't seem to be able to avoid it, do we?'

Next moment Jules hurried in, sweating and out of breath. 'No sign of your friends,' he reported sadly. 'I've left the front door unlatched.'

Ian looked uneasy. 'So anyone can walk in,' he muttered to Barbara in English.

Jules caught the gist of the remark. 'Please try to be patient,' he pleaded. 'I know what it is like. I have done my share of waiting too.'

Barbara bit her lip and cleared her throat. 'Jules . . . when I said those things before . . . about making judgements of people . . . ' She trailed into embarrassed silence, searching for the appropriate words in French.

Jules smiled understandingly. 'You said things because of Léon Colbert, the man,' he said kindly. 'But I had to deal with what Léon Colbert represented. Barbara, do you ever wonder why I do these things . . . Hiding in alleyways and dark corners . . . Fighting in the shadows . . . ?'

Ian looked up. 'We assume that you and Jean belong to the aristocracy. You are Royalists.'

Jules shook his head very firmly. 'I have no title, no special status. I am a *bourgeois* – somewhere in the middle . . . ' He sat down between them, desperate to make them understand. 'I hate to see order swept up like dust and thrown carelessly out of the window. That is the Terror: there can be no loyalty or honour when anarchy reigns . . . '

Barbara nodded as if she understood. 'And Léon was your friend.'

Jules shrugged miserably. 'My sister Danielle always suspected him,' he revealed. 'There are only two sides today: those who rule by fear and treachery, and those who fight for reason and decency. Anybody who betrays us is worse than the Devil in Hell.'

Jules fell silent as the front door slammed shut. They all rose and turned to the door of the dining room.

'At last, they're here!' Ian breathed.

The door opened and the Doctor walked in followed by Lemaître.

'Lemaître!' gasped Barbara, her smile of joy crumpling into an appalled grimace.

Jules's mouth fell open as he stared at Lemaître and then at the Doctor. 'Worse than the Devil in Hell . . . ' he repeated, turning to the dumbfounded young English couple. 'Your friend, the Doctor . . . he has betrayed us!' Jules snatched out a pistol and trained it at Lemaître's head. Slowly Lemaître raised his hands in the air.

All at once, there was a stir in the street outside and Ian rushed across to peer through the shutters.

'They've brought the soldiers . . . ' he warned.

Lemaître shook his head emphatically. 'No! We come alone and unarmed,' he declared. 'Ask your friend here.'

The Doctor nodded gravely. 'It is true. I made a bargain with Lemaître. Let him speak. He is holding Susan hostage in the *Conciergerie*.'

Jules gazed contemptuously at Lemaître. 'What can you possibly have to say to us?' he sneered, keeping his pistol levelled.

Lemaître kept his hands high above his head. 'Please Renan, I came here as a friend,' he protested.

'*A friend*!' Barbara exclaimed sarcastically.

Lemaître turned to Ian. 'Chesterton will confirm that what I say is true,' he claimed.

Ian turned from the window. '*I* will?' he echoed in disbelief.

Lemaître smiled. 'Surely you realised that your escape from the *Conciergerie* was planned? I ensured that you got the key to your cell and I took care of the gaoler,' he revealed.

Ian frowned sceptically. 'But why? Why should you do that for me?'

131

Lemaître stepped forward. 'I was certain that Webster gave you a message to deliver to me, but I had to be sure. So I gave you the opportunity . . . But time is running short now . . .'

The others all stared at Lemaître as he slowly lowered his arms.

'Yes,' he announced in perfect English. 'I am James Stirling.'

Ian uttered a mirthless laugh of derision. 'You? *You* are James Stirling . . . ?'

The tall, noble figure shrugged. 'Is it really so surprising, Ian? You must realise that to be of any use at all James Stirling would have to hold a position of authority.'

Ian looked unconvinced. 'But if you're Stirling, why didn't you ask Webster to give you his message himself before he died?'

Stirling smiled patiently. 'It was not safe for me to make myself known . . . to break my cover . . .' he explained. 'But now circumstances are changing rapidly and I need to move fast.'

Jules had struggled to follow the incredible revelations in English. 'If you are Stirling why have you not made yourself known to us here?' he demanded suspiciously. 'Webster knew about me.'

Stirling spread his hands as if acknowledging how unlikely his story must sound. 'I had to create an absolutely credible existence as Lemaître,' he claimed earnestly. 'I could trust no-one. I have been close to the very highest people.' Stirling lowered his voice. 'I enjoy the confidence of Robespierre himself.'

'He does,' confirmed the Doctor.

But Ian was still not satisfied. 'You could have made yourself known to me in prison,' he insisted.

Stirling sighed and shook his head. 'There are spies everywhere. I could trust no-one,' he repeated adamantly.

The Doctor suddenly decided to assert his presence. 'All very interesting, Stirling . . . Lemaître . . . whatever your name is,' he interrupted rudely. 'However, the only reason I brought you here was to help my granddaughter. I've kept my part of the bargain.'

Stirling nodded. 'I know, but you must permit me to explain my position . . .'

The Doctor made everybody jump by banging his stick on the floor several times. 'I most certainly will not!' he shouted cantankerously. 'I want Susan out of prison immediately!'

Stirling restrained himself as best he could. 'I will help you if you will help me,' he declared, trying hard not to antagonise the irascible old man. 'Don't you see? I can use my influence to guarantee you a safe passage . . . wherever you want to go.'

Ian and Barbara exchanged glances. 'Stirling's right, Doctor,' Ian suggested gently. Stirling's promise of a safe passage to wherever they wished to go had suddenly sounded very attractive to the two travel-weary humans.

The Doctor grunted and wandered over to the window to take advantage of a slight but unmistakably cool breeze that had just sprung up. His Time Lord metabolism had been suffering cruelly in the humid heat, especially under his heavy ceremonial finery.

'I promise you, no harm will befall Susan,' Stirling added. 'I gave orders that she was to remain in the cell.'

The Doctor's nostrils flared. 'I hardly regard the gaoler as the ideal custodian of my granddaughter,' he retorted crossly.

'The gaoler would die sooner than allow that cell door to be opened without my orders,' Stirling assured him.

The Doctor took several deep gulps of refreshing breeze wafting through the shutters. He knew he had to give way, but he was reluctant to admit it. 'Very well, Stirling, tell your story if you must . . .' he sighed.

Jules sat down to listen, but kept his pistol on his knees just in case. Barbara and Ian stood nearby.

Stirling turned eagerly to Ian. 'The message,' he requested. 'First give me Webster's message.'

Ian hesitated. 'Well, Webster told me very little. He was badly wounded as you know . . .'

Stirling nodded impatiently. 'Yes, Ian, I read all the reports of arrests in case something like that happened. That was why I came to your cell. I'd been expecting Webster to contact me for several weeks.'

Ian still didn't look convinced. 'But Webster didn't know where you were or how I could find you.'

Stirling's noble face betrayed mounting frustration. 'Ian . . . The message!' he urged.

Ian glanced at Jules and Barbara. They both nodded.

'All right. Webster said that you were to return to England immediately,' Ian informed him. 'It seems that whatever information you may have is urgently needed there.'

Stirling nodded and waited for Ian to continue. Ian shrugged. 'That's all he said.'

Stirling looked deeply disappointed. 'Are you sure?'

Ian thought back. 'Yes . . . Oh, he did mumble a few words when he was losing consciousness, but I've told you everything he asked me to tell you.'

Stirling went up to Ian and searched his face in desperation. 'What were the mumblings about, Ian? Please try to remember.'

'Just odd words . . . ' Ian recalled vaguely. 'They didn't make any sense. I'm sure he would have told me if they were important.'

James Stirling looked across the room at the Doctor's back. 'Well, I've already started planning my return to England,' he revealed. 'But before I can go and before I can give Susan and the rest of you a safe passage, there is one more piece of information I must have.'

Barbara looked deeply puzzled. 'You asked for our help. But what can we do? You are the one with all the power,' she pointed out.

Stirling glanced at Jules. 'Robespierre sent for me today. There is·another plot to depose him.'

Jules had been following the discussion in English as closely as he could. 'Good!' he exclaimed, his eyes lighting up. 'Will it succeed this time?'

Stirling stared back at the Doctor's aloof figure, as if he did not trust him. 'Possibly, Jules,' he replied. 'The First Deputy instructed me to follow Paul Barras to a secret rendezvous and to report personally to him on what is said at the meeting.'

Suddenly Ian struck himself on the forehead with his fist.

'Barras! A meeting . . . ' he echoed, beginning to remember. 'Webster mentioned that to me.'

Stirling swung round and grasped him by the shoulders. 'What did Webster say?' he demanded, his eyes blazing with urgency.

Ian pulled a face and bit his lip as he made an enormous effort to recall the dying man's exact words. 'It was nothing specific . . . He mentioned Barras and . . . and a ship . . . He kept talking about a sinking ship . . . The Sinking Ship . . . That was it . . . A name of some kind . . . '

Jules sprang to his feet, almost dropping his pistol. '*The Sinking Ship*! There is an inn of that name on the Calais Road!' he cried excitedly. 'I know it. It is a lonely place, ideal for a secret meeting.'

Stirling's face seemed to shed a massive, oppressive weight. 'Perhaps we could arrange for the meeting to be overheard . . . ' he speculated. 'Once I know the purpose of that meeting I shall be ready to return to England . . . And free to help you all.'

'Do you know who Barras intends to meet?' asked Barbara, trying to remember her French history.

Stirling shook his head. 'Whoever it is, it could be the next ruler of France,' he declared dramatically.

Ian opened his mouth to suggest a probable name but was silenced by a sudden sharp warning glance from the Doctor, who had abruptly swung round from the window. Ian coughed and smiled sheepishly. 'I still can't see how we can help you,' he told Stirling.

'Barras knows me by sight,' Stirling explained. 'My plan, if you agree, is for you and Barbara to "attend" the meeting, so to speak.'

'Out of the question!' declared the Doctor, striding into the centre of the room, his plumes waving magnificently. 'The risk is far too great.'

Jules intervened. 'Why not use your own people?' he asked.

Stirling clasped his temples as if in despair of ever making them understand. 'I have no-one. I work alone,' he replied wearily. 'It is the only way. Then only James Stirling can betray James Stirling.'

135

The others were strangely impressed by this simple and honest statement and by Stirling's air of dedicated courage. Barbara moved closer to Ian. 'I think we should help,' she murmured.

Ian saw that she was fired by the same curiosity as he was himself. He nodded enthusiastically.

The Doctor saw that they were determined to get involved. 'Very well,' he agreed. 'It's risky, but we do have Susan's welfare to consider.'

Stirling seized Ian's and Barbara's arms. 'Then you agree to go?'

'We agree,' Barbara grinned.

Stirling heaved a tremendous sigh of relief. 'The Doctor and I will remain here,' he decided. 'If we were seen it could be disastrous.'

Jules had replaced his pistol in his pocket. 'I will escort Ian and Barbara to the rendezvous, Stirling, if you are not objecting,' he proposed in halting English.

Stirling smiled gratefully. 'Thank you, Jules. I was about to suggest it myself.'

The Frenchman hurried to the cabinet and took out a map which he spread on the dining table. 'It is a ride of a good two hours,' he told them as they gathered round. 'We take the Calais road north until this wood. Then we turn left and ride to the west . . . '

'You shouldn't have any trouble reaching the inn tonight,' Stirling told them. 'Stay the night and return in the morning. That way you will be less likely to meet any patrols.'

The Doctor sniffed doubtfully as he studied the map over Ian's and Barbara's shoulders. He was clearly unhappy about the plan, but he realised that Susan's future depended entirely upon Stirling obtaining what he wanted. He also knew that terrestrial history depended on it too . . . And he was forbidden to interfere with history.

Stirling sat down at the table in a business-like mood. 'Now, I suggest you take care of the innkeeper first . . . ' he began.

Ian raised his hand. 'Don't worry, Stirling, you can leave everything to us,' he assured him, nodding at Barbara and Jules.

Stirling laughed. 'Of course. Forgive me, but this could be the most vital operation in my whole mission here,' he admitted. 'I don't want it to fail.'

'Neither do I!' remarked the Doctor drily, with a significant wink at Ian and Barbara. 'So let's make sure it doesn't, shall we?'

11

A Glimpse Of Things To Come

The rotting wooden sign of *The Sinking Ship* inn creaked violently in the fiercely gusting wind. Thick storm clouds raced across the pale moon and the rain lashed this way and that in drenching curtains across the deserted countryside. The bleak, rolling hills resembled monstrous waves in a troubled sea and the dilapidated inn certainly looked like a sinking ship. It was almost as gloomy inside, deep shadows falling between the feeble pools of light cast by one or two guttering oil lamps. The bare floorboards and rough timber walls of the low-ceilinged bar were very unwelcoming, and there were only a couple of shady customers crouched over their wineglasses in the grubby little alcove seats, listening to the lash of the rain and the hiss of the wind around the edges of the door.

Muffled in a greatcoat, with a tricorn hat pulled down over his eyes, Jules Renan sat alone watching the rain trickle down the filthy panes and occasionally glancing warily at the other two customers. He looked up as Barbara brought over a bottle and a glass on a tray and set them down in front of him. She was wearing a crinkly-edged mobcap over her thick dark hair and a plain dress with a shawl and a bib.

'Thank you, Barbara,' Jules muttered in French, tossing a few coins onto her tray.

Barbara scratched her head under the itchy cap and yawned. 'If this is a typical night's trade I'm not surprised this place was chosen for a secret meeting,' she said, picking up the coins.

Jules grinned under his hat. 'I hope I gagged the inn-keeper securely enough. We do not want him yelling up from the cellar and spoiling everything.'

There was a sudden clinking sound from among the bottles haphazardly arranged on the lopsided shelving behind the bar. Jules and Barbara glanced quickly across at the other customers and then back at each other.

'Ian must be through . . . ' Barbara murmured nervously.

Jules nodded and poured himself some wine.

'If Barras leaves it much longer he will find the place closed,' Barbara remarked, picking up her tray.

Jules shrugged. 'Perhaps that is what he is waiting for.'

Barbara strolled casually back to the bar, collecting a few empty glasses from the tables on the way. She set the tray down on the counter and turned, pretending to arrange the bottles on the shelves behind her. Level with her eyes she saw a sharp threaded spike, like the tip of a drill, sticking out of the wall from the other side. Stealthily she moved a bottle that was in danger of being knocked off the shelf by the revolving tool. Again she glanced at the customers in the alcove seats and was relieved that they seemed totally oblivious of the furtive activity in the small private room next door.

Humming nonchalantly to herself to conceal her uneasi-ness, Barbara opened the door at the side of the bar and slipped quietly into the neighbouring room.

She found Ian Chesterton - wearing the innkeeper's floppy brimmed hat, calico shirt and leather apron - standing beside the wall separating the private room from the bar. He was carefully turning the handle of a large awl, and boring a hole about a centimetre in diameter in the wooden planking behind some bookshelves.

'You're through, Ian,' she told him, closing the door behind her.

'Good. I'm just enlarging the hole a little bit,' Ian replied. 'Many out there now?'

'Just two apart from Jules. I don't think they'll stay much longer. The storm's getting worse.'

Ian gingerly removed the sharp end of the awl from the wall and squinted through the hole into the bar. 'We're all set then,' he murmured. 'Now all we have to do is get rid of the clientele somehow.'

Barbara nodded. 'Jules says the innkeeper shouldn't give us any trouble?'

Ian replaced several books around the hole so that it was not obstructed but also not visible except to someone who knew it was there. Then he made a quick check around the sparsely-furnished little room to make sure that everything was in order for the secret meeting. 'Come on, Barbara . . . ' he said, leading the way back into the bar. 'Everything's ready now.'

No sooner had they closed the door to the private room than the outer door burst open in a flurry of rain and wind and a soaking wet figure strode into the dimly-lit bar. As the newcomer slammed the door against the turbulent night, Jules Renan gave a furtive signal with his little finger.

Catching Jules's sign, Ian hurried to greet the windblown visitor. 'Allow me to take your cloak, Citizen . . . ' he said respectfully in a gruff voice, hoping that his crude accent would be accepted as the local idiom.

Paul Barras hesitated for a second and Barbara felt a cold wave of panic sweep over her in case their deception had been discovered because of some glaring mistake.

'Where is Monsieur Jacques?' Barras demanded in a deep bass voice, removing his hat with its tricolour cockade.

Ian thought quickly. 'Jacques sends his sincere apologies, Citizen. He has been stricken with fever. He asked me and my good wife here to take care of things in his absence.' Ian took Barras's hat. 'You must be the Citizen who reserved the private room. Everything is ready for you.'

Barras stared around the bar. He had a square, heavy face with fleshy jowls and sunken eyes slightly too close together. His long brown hair was gathered in a large bow of ribbon at the back. He wore a huge tricolour sash across his chest under a severely square-cut coat. Removing his enormous cloak, he handed it to Ian and then strode through into the private room followed by Barbara.

Barras glanced briefly around the small room furnished with a rug, a table and a few chairs. Then he went over to look out of the window, as if to make sure that there were no spies lurking outside. Apparently satisfied, he approached the bookshelves and began to leaf through the handful of dusty volumes. As his browsing brought him nearer and nearer to the hole gouged by Ian, Barbara edged nervously up to him.

'Can I bring the Citizen some refreshment?' she inquired with a respectful smile.

Barras turned and moved to the table. 'Yes, a bottle of wine and two glasses,' he replied.

'Is the Citizen expecting many guests?' Barbara asked, trying to judge whether Barras had spotted the hole or not.

Barras glared at her. 'Two glasses,' he repeated, as if the answer were obvious.

Barbara nodded and did a sort of fumbled curtsey. 'Of course, Citizen . . . ' she murmured, hurrying out to the bar.

Ian had been making a great performance of clearing empty bottles and washing glasses at the bar and at last the two furtive customers had taken the hint. They put on their hats and shuffled out, nodding goodnight to Jules and slamming the door.

Barbara put a fresh bottle of wine and two clean glasses on her tray. 'There will just be the two of them apparently,' she told Ian before hurrying back to the private room.

Ian nodded to Jules, signalling that it was time for him to depart. Jules drained his glass after raising it in a silent toast of good luck. Then he stood up and went out into the storm. Ian peered cautiously through the hole in the wall behind the bar and watched Barbara place the tray in front of Barras.

Barras inspected the bottle and the clean glasses carefully while Barbara hovered nearby.

'Will there be anything else, Citizen?' she inquired.

Barras glanced at his fob watch. 'No,' he grunted. 'My guest should arrive very soon. Just make sure we are not disturbed.'

Barbara curtsied. 'Of course, Citizen,' she smiled and hurried out, leaving Barras walking restlessly round and round the table.

'As soon as his guest arrives you can lock up,' Ian told her as she rejoined him at the bar. 'I'll keep an eye on what goes on next door.'

While Barbara flitted nervously around doing unnecessary tidying up, Ian made one last check to make sure he had a good view of the private room through the wall. Fortunately, Barras had not obscured the hole when he replaced the books.

After what felt like an interminable delay, they heard the jangle of harnesses and the rumble of wheels in the muddy yard outside. Ian squeezed Barbara's trembling hand and they stood at the bar with their eyes fixed on the outside door. Meanwhile the door to the private room opened and Paul Barras waited impatiently for his visitor. There was a splash of boots across the yard and the door flew open with a bang.

In swept a short, muffled figure wearing the uniform of a Brigadier-General. A tall triangular hat pulled well down and a voluminous cape and muffler concealed most of his face, except for a pair of intense brown eyes. Barbara hurried over to shut and bolt the door.

Barras came forward to great the stranger. 'I am delighted that you were able to get here,' he smiled. 'Please come this way.' And he ushered the muffled figure into the small room and shut the door.

Barbara ran across to Ian. 'Did you recognise who it was?' she asked breathlessly.

'No. Did you?'

Barbara shook her head and nodded at the tiny spy-hole.

Just as Ian was about to take a peek, the door to the private room suddenly opened again and the stranger stared intently around the bar before going back inside and shutting the door.

Ian waited for a few moments and then he cautiously put his eye to the hole. What he witnessed in the following seconds made him gasp in astonishment. Next door, the stranger had removed his hat, greatcoat and muffler. As the man turned to face Paul Barras, Ian found himself squinting at the twenty-five year old Corsican warrior, Napoleon Bonaparte.

'Barbara . . . Barbara, it's . . . it's Napoleon!' Ian whispered, almost loudly enough to be heard in the next room. 'It's Napoleon Bonaparte!'

Barbara flung down her dishcloth and Ian made way for her to take a look. She saw the squat, almost neckless figure, as if in a portrait come miraculously to life. There was the famous fringe brushed forward over the high forehead, the twin curls in front of the ears, the arched nose and the small, rather mean mouth. The gold braid on his collar and epaulettes and the broad sash knotted around his waist gave Napoleon an impressive air despite his short stature. For Barbara, the only disappointment was the fact that the future First Consul and Emperor of France did not have his hand tucked into the opposite flap of his tunic.

'It's history in the making . . . ' Barbara whispered, reluctantly moving aside to allow Ian to eavesdrop and obtain the information James Stirling so desperately wanted in exchange for Susan's safe release.

Bonaparte sat down opposite Barras at the table and pulled off his gloves. 'The meeting place was ideally chosen,' he declared in heavily-accented French.

Barras nodded. 'We are quite secure here. I made certain I was not followed.' He offered his guest wine.

Napoleon shook his head resolutely.

Barras poured himself a glass. 'General, may I assume that your presence here signifies that you are interested in my proposition?' he inquired.

Napoleon's face remained expressionless. 'Interested, but no more than that,' he agreed, 'until I have all the details.'

Barras drank some wine. 'Robespierre will be arrested after tomorrow's meeting of the Convention,' he revealed.

Bonaparte's mouth twitched sceptically. 'Will be?' he echoed mockingly. 'It will not be the first attempt.'

'This time it will not fail,' Barras assured him. 'He will be tried and executed before his associates can react.'

Napoleon smiled faintly. 'You make it sound so very simple, Barras. But I fear you underestimate Robespierre. He has a talent for survival.'

It was Barras's turn to smile. 'Only if he is allowed to speak, General. And he will not be,' he promised.

There was a pause. Napoleon rose and went to stare out of the window at the tempest raging outside the inn. 'As far as I am concerned, your success or failure mean very little,' he declared coldly. 'I am a soldier and I am about to leave for Constantinople to reorganise the Turkish artillery . . .'

Barras rose to confront the lukewarm Corsican. 'I am well aware of your contempt for us politicians, tearing France to pieces while the Allies prepare to pounce . . .' he began.

Napoleon raised his hand in a commanding gesture. 'Exactly what is your proposal?' he demanded.

Barras sipped his wine. 'To govern France successfully, General, I believe that one needs the support of the majority of the governed,' he said earnestly.

Napoleon nodded impatiently. 'And after destroying Robespierre, how do you propose to gain that support?'

'With you, General,' Barras replied, smiling and sipping his wine. 'Your recent triumphs in the Austrian Camapign have made you a hero in the People's eyes.'

Bonaparte shrugged. 'And in *your* eyes, Citizen Barras?'

Barras remained silent, trying to think of a diplomatic response. It was no secret that the Corsican General had irritated the Government with his spirited independence of mind and had even spent a few days under house arrest.

Napoleon's eyes gleamed shrewdly. 'A useful prop for your new Revolutionary Government?' he suggested ironically.

Barras uttered an embarrassed laugh. 'Oh, come, come, General, you would be much more than a mere figurehead,' he said hastily.

The Corsican turned sharply. 'I am glad you appreciate that fact,' he said modestly. 'In what capacity would I be required to serve the Revolution?'

'We shall amend the Constitution,' Barras answered hurriedly, as if it would be done there and then. 'The amendment will provide for government by three Consuls. You, General will be one of them.'

There was a brief pause.

'When do you require my decision?'

'At once.'

'And if I refuse?'

Barras stared into his wine glass. 'You are in a strong position, General, but you are not completely indispensable . . . ' he replied carefully. 'There are other ambitious young men . . . '

Bonaparte raised his hand again as if he were halting a marching column. 'You will not need them. I accept,' he said sharply.

Barras's dour face broke into a sunny smile of triumph and relief. But before he could reply, Bonaparte went on.

'I accept, subject to Robespierre's downfall,' he stipulated. 'If your coup fails, I shall deny this meeting ever took place and depart at once for Constantinople.'

Barras nodded his eager agreement. 'I will summon you to Paris as soon as a suitable time has elapsed.'

Napoleon Bonaparte picked up his gloves and his hat and faced the much older and more powerful politician squarely, with a dash of youthful arrogance in his confident stare. 'I shall be ready to take over . . . ' he said with prophetic certainty.

On the other side of the wall, Ian and Barbara exchanged wry glances at Barras's disconcerted reaction, barely able to appreciate fully the fact that they were eavesdropping on a momentous historical event. Their excitement made them careless.

'Poor old Barras doesn't know what he's letting France in for!' Barbara couldn't help chuckling.

Next moment they both dodged away from the wall as the door to the private room burst open and the future dictator of France strode out into the bar pulling on his greatcoat and smiling with the blessing of destiny on his sallow features.

'Bonaparte?' Napoleon Bonaparte the ruler of France?' James Stirling stared incredulously at Ian and Barbara as the early morning sunshine streamed into Jules Renan's dining room.

'As one of three Consuls,' Barbara repeated patiently for the umpteenth time.

Stirling laughed hollowly as he paced up and down the room between them. 'He won't be content with being one of three,' he predicted grimly. 'I've watched his promotion . . . Bonaparte is clever and ambitious. He intends to rule alone and one day he will, just you wait and see!'

Ian was tempted to say that they didn't need to wait and see, but a warning glance from the Doctor kept him silent.

The Doctor, who had remained silent by the window while Ian and Barbara had related what they had heard and seen at the inn, suddenly roused himself and strode into the middle of the room shaking his walking stick impatiently. 'Our only concern now is Susan,' he announced sternly.

James Stirling shook his head. 'Susan is only one of our concerns, Doctor,' he objected. 'If Robespierre is arrested and taken to the *Conciergerie*, we might find it impossible to get in there, let alone get your granddaughter safely out.'

Ian stepped forward angrily. 'We made a bargain, Stirling!'

'And I'll keep to it, Ian,' Stirling pledged.

'You must have suspected that this might happen, Stirling,' the Doctor accused him, his hollow face lined with anxiety about Susan's perilous situation.

The English intelligence agent frowned in dismay. 'I did, but I had no idea Barras was so strong,' he admitted. He turned to Jules who had also kept silent since their return from the inn. 'Jules, what time is the Convention meeting?' he asked, a note of desperation creeping into his robust voice.

Jules glanced at the clock. 'It would be ended by now,' he replied in his hesitant English.

Stirling picked up his hat from the table. 'Then Robespierre may already be in custody,' he said. 'But there may still be time . . . I must find out.'

As he picked up his cane and moved to the door, Barbara rushed forward and clasped his arm. 'You mean, you'd try to keep Robespierre as ruler of France?' she exclaimed in disbelief.

Stirling stared fiercely into her eyes. 'If I were convinced it was the only way to prevent outright war between England

and France, I'd have no choice,' he confessed. 'Am I right, Jules?'

Jules Renan nodded unhappily and turned to Barbara. 'We need a strong government – but not a military dictatorship . . . ' he told her earnestly. 'And a military tyranny could happen . . . '

'But it *will* happen!' Barbara cried, unable to appreciate that Jules and Stirling could not foresee what she already knew. 'You can't change history . . . '

The Doctor eased Barbara gently away from Stirling's side. 'My dear Miss Wright, it's no use. You're wasting your breath,' he chided her, like a kindly headmaster in the staff room. 'They will have to wait until it is time for them to know the truth . . . ' He turned to Stirling and Renan. 'Do as you think fit. I'm going to free Susan,' he declared defiantly, brandishing his stick.

James Stirling bowed to the inevitable. 'Take Barbara with you,' he suggested, in a sudden rush of words. 'Let her wait outside the *Conciergerie*. Jules, you obtain a carriage and horses and meet Barbara outside the prison. If the Doctor can get Susan out, they will join Barbara and wait for you. Ian and I will join you all as soon as we can.'

Ian grabbed Stirling's sleeve as Jules hurried out. 'And where are *we* going?' he demanded.

'To Robespierre's chamber,' Stirling replied, putting on his hat. 'As Citizen Lemaître I may be able to delay things to give the Doctor a little more time.' He turned to the Doctor. 'If you are not waiting outside the prison when we arrive, we shall come in to find you . . . ' he promised.

Confused and weary after the long night's exploits, Ian looked to the Doctor for guidance as Stirling strode to the door and waited there impatiently for everyone to respond to his plan.

'Yes, do as he says Chesterton,' the Doctor reluctantly agreed after a moment's consideration. 'You can't really help me, but you can help to make sure that our friend Stirling or Lemaître or whoever he is turns up to help us get away.'

Ian nodded. 'Okay, Doctor. See you outside the prison. Good luck everybody.'

Barbara ran over and kissed his cheek. 'Take good care, Ian,' she murmured, squeezing his arm.

Ian and James Stirling strode away, leaving the Doctor and Barbara suddenly alone. Barbara unexpectedly broke into a fit of giggling which made her eyes water and her nose run.

The Doctor seized her arm and shook her, anxious to be on his way to rescue Susan. 'What on earth is the matter, young woman?' he demanded. 'What do you find so very amusing?'

Barbara did her best to pull herself together. 'It's all this . . . all this activity to try and prevent something happening that we know is inevitable . . . ' she giggled, wiping her eyes. 'I mean, Robespierre *will* be arrested and guillotined, whatever we do or don't do.'

The Doctor frowned as if he failed to see the joke. 'Of course, my dear. I have explained the situation to you often enough during our travels. We cannot change or influence history . . . '

Barbara instantly became serious. 'I learned that lesson during our visit to the Aztecs . . . ' she recalled wryly.

The Doctor led her firmly towards the door. 'Everything will take place just as it was recorded,' he confirmed. 'We cannot influence the tide . . . but we can stop ourselves being swept away in the flood of events.'

Barbara's eyes darkened with doubt. 'Oh my goodness . . . Susan!' she cried, grabbing the Doctor's arm and dragging him along. 'Come on, Doctor, we don't have time to philosophise. We've got to get to the prison!'

12

Escaping from History

The Convention meeting had disintegrated in uproar and
Robespierre had been forced to flee from the throng of angry
Deputies clamouring for his resignation, and worse, his
removal from office. Reaching his chamber, he bolted the
double doors and leaned against them panting for breath and
tugging loose his torn and dishevelled cravat and collar.

After a few seconds, a sudden thought seemed to fill him
with panic. Rushing to his ornate desk, he started rummaging in the drawers and among the bundles of documents
scattered everywhere. In his haste he flung papers in all
directions in a frenzy of desperation. At last his green eyes
lighted on the document he sought. Folding it, he stuffed it
into an inner pocket of his sky blue silk coat and then leaned
on the desk, his lungs heaving under his thin chest.

Next moment a cacophony of shouts and a couple of
gunshots cracked the forbidding silence in the anteroom
outside. Robespierre snatched a pistol out of the drawer,
checked that it was loaded and cocked and hastened to look
out of the long windows overlooking the courtyard. Then he
ran over to check the bolts on the doors. Finally he backed
away behind the desk, still breathing hard, the sweat
glistening on his sickly complexion like the tacky bloom on
waxed fruit as he listened to the relentless approach of
tramping boots and shouting deputies.

'This is the tyrant's lair!' yelled a voice on the other side of
the doors as the handles were seized and wrenched violently
to and fro. 'Open up, Robespierre . . . Down with tyranny

. . . The Terror is finished . . . Long live France . . . !' The yells were punctuated by the crash of musket butts against the doors.

The First Deputy stood behind his desk, levelling his pistol at the shuddering doors, his whole body quaking with fear. All at once the panelling split, the doors gave way and a motley crowd of soldiers, deputies and *sans-culottes* burst into the chamber, cheering and brandishing an assortment of weaponry.

Their leader ceremonially unrolled a document. 'Citizen Robespierre, I have here a warrant for your arrest issued by the Committee of Public Safety . . . ' he proclaimed loudly. The announcement was cheered with bloodthirsty enthusiasm.

Robespierre stood his ground. 'Traitors! They are all of them traitors!' he shrieked. 'Do not be fools. They will never succeed in taking over the People's government. They failed to arrest me in the Convention just now! They failed!'

His hysterical taunts inflamed the mob even more. They leered expectantly at their trembling victim and advanced a few paces, forcing him back against the windows.

'Within a few hours I shall be as secure as ever . . . ' Robespierre boasted, his weak voice cracking with emotion. 'The traitors will pay with their lives. Do not let them make use of you. If you swear your allegiance to me now you will all be safe. I will guarantee . . . '

'Allegiance? Sounds like the old King all over again!' scoffed one of the soldiers.

Next moment a shot rang out, deafening everybody. Robespierre flung his pistol against the ceiling and clutched at his mouth as blood, teeth and fragments of jawbone spurted out between his clawing fingers. As his pistol hit the ceiling it discharged, shattering the elegant chandelier so that glass splinters cascaded all over him to the delight of the laughing and gesticulating crowd.

'That'll keep him quiet . . . We'll get no more lip from him!' quipped the leader, rolling up his warrant and motioning two soldiers to seize their hideously wounded victim. 'Come on, Citizen. You're wanted at the *Conciergerie*!'

The jeering, jostling posse dragged the wild-eyed,

moaning First Deputy out of the chamber. In the anteroom, Ian Chesterton and James Stirling stood among the crowd, watching in horrified fascination as the Tyrant of France was manhandled brutally past them, a horrific scarlet foam flecked with teeth bubbling between his cupped hands.

'You should have let me go in there, Ian,' Stirling muttered, his face white with shock.

'We were too late,' Ian argued, his hand covering his mouth as he felt the urge to vomit overwhelm him. 'Robespierre is finished now.'

Stirling nodded grimly. 'Tyranny is dead, long live tyranny. They are taking him to the *Conciergerie* . . . We shall have to hurry.'

Ian stared after the jubilant captors. 'It's up to the Doctor now,' he muttered apprehensively.

All at once there was a tremendous clap of thunder. Outside the windows, the sky had darkened again.

Opposite the main gates of the *Conciergerie*, the Doctor and Barbara were pressed into the shadows under a jutting porch which afforded them some shelter from the storm as well as protection from the gathering crowds in the street. Behind them, the deserted building had been boarded up and glass from broken windows littered the ground.

'There's going to be quite a storm,' muttered the Doctor, glancing at the forbidding black clouds banked up over the dangerously tense city.

Barbara drew her shawl more closely around her, not to keep warm, but as a token defence. 'You can feel the electricity in the air,' she agreed, eyeing the jostling, excited crowds that had begun to collect as soon as the rumours of Robespierre's fate had started to spread.

A searing flash of lightning was accompanied simultaneously by an ear-splitting crash of thunder.

'It's directly overhead,' remarked the Doctor, bracing himself for the ordeal ahead of him. 'We've waited long enough. Jules should have arrived with the transport when I get back with Susan. Will you be all right, Barbara?'

Barbara swallowed nervously. 'Yes, of course I will,' she lied bravely. 'Go and find Susan, Doctor.'

The Doctor smiled gravely and adjusted his plumed hat to a more authoritative angle. 'I'll try, my dear, I'll try . . . ' he promised, moving out cautiously into the street and barging his way through the crowd to rap on the gate with his stick.

The gaoler, who had been sharing a celebratory drink with a couple of guards in his alcove, rose slowly to his feet gawping in amazement as the Doctor strode up to the table un-announced.

'You! You came back!' he stuttered, wiping his mouth with his mucky sleeve.

The Doctor smiled condescendingly. 'I see that you did not expect me, gaoler.'

The startled gaoler rattled his keys expectantly. 'No, I didn't but I'm glad you're here because I've-got a score to settle with you . . . ' he growled.

The Doctor threw back his head and stared coldly down his nose at the belching, befuddled fool. 'So you have not yet heard the news?' he declared.

The gaoler snorted derisively. 'Who hasn't? Robes-pierre's been ditched.'

The Doctor nodded solemnly. 'And Lemaître's been shot while trying to escape,' he said harshly.

The gaoler hesitated, screwing up his bulbous face like a wrinkled melon. 'Lemaître shot . . . ?' he croaked uneasily.

The Doctor's plumes nodded impressively. 'Shot. And now we are going to deal with his accomplices,' he announced in a hard voice.

The gaoler shook his head vigorously as if trying to shake the drink out of his brain. 'Who *are* you?' he asked tentatively.

'Exactly,' rapped the Doctor. He walked round the swaying drunkard, poking him in the stomach with the end of his walking stick. 'Why do you imagine such a high-ranking official as myself came to Paris? I was a vital participant in the plan to oust the tyrant Robespierre,' he explained in a severe, hectoring tone.

The gaoler fiddled sheepishly with his keys. 'I . . . I didn't know, Citizen . . . ' he cringed, all his swaggering bravado gone.

The Doctor slashed at the table with his stick, sending papers, mugs and bottles flying. 'No, you didn't, did you!' he shouted. 'And that's why you didn't expect me to come back, isn't it! You thought you'd be able to get away with it!'

The trembling gaoler glanced apprehensively at the two soldiers who were staring open-mouthed at the Doctor. 'Get away with what, Citizen?' he whimpered pathetically.

'With being Lemaître's accomplice!' the Doctor shouted ruthlessly. 'Guards! Seize the villain!'

Startled out of their wits, the two young militiamen each grabbed one of the cowering gaoler's arms.

The Doctor continued to pace round and round them, slapping his stick violently on the table. 'You *were* Lemaître's accomplice, weren't you!' he stormed in an outraged tone. 'You assisted him in carrying out his treacherous crimes!'

The gaoler was on the brink of tears now. He winced as the Doctor's accusations were reinforced by the thunderstorm overhead. 'But Citizen, I only carried out the orders I was given . . . ' he pleaded.

The Doctor stopped in front of him and thrust his harsh features right into the gaoler's sweating face. 'Only carrying out orders?' he echoed contemptuously. 'That is the cowardly cliché trotted out by inhuman sadists throughout history,' he hissed, his eyes burning with utter disdain. 'I was here, remember? I saw you conniving with Lemaître the whole time.'

'But I wasn't . . . I wasn't, Citizen . . . ' the gaoler stuttered, really frightened now.

'Wasn't what?'

The quaking bully hesitated. 'Con . . . Whatever you said I was,' he squawked.

The Doctor paused dramatically. 'Was it not you who betrayed me to him? Betrayed *me*?' he accused menacingly.

The gaoler's courage rallied a little. 'Well, you did hit me on the head, didn't you,' he pointed out. 'And how was I to know Lemaître was a traitor . . . And that you, Citizen, were . . . ' He paused cunningly. 'I mean, after all that was a secret, wasn't it . . . ?'

The Doctor paced thoughtfully for a few minutes. 'There is some logic in what you say,' he admitted. 'You may be just a foolish rogue and not be aware of it,' he said with an indulgent smile. 'I am prepared to give you the benefit of the doubt. While we are reconsidering the position of gaoler here, I shall allow you to remain in a temporary capacity.'

The flushed, sweating gaoler swallowed hard and sighed with immense relief as the Doctor motioned the soldiers to release him. 'Thank you . . . Thank you, Citizen. You will not regret your generosity,' he promised.

'I should hope not, for your sake!' the Doctor warned. 'Now, listen to me. Robespierre was smuggled out of the Convention, but the militia will catch him and probably bring him here.'

The gaoler rubbed his leathery hands. 'We'll take good care of him, Citizen, never fear,' he vowed.

The Doctor raised his hand. 'Later there will be a whole new consignment of prisoners as Robespierre's treacherous associates are rounded up. You had better have the cells emptied and made ready for them,' he ordered.

The gaoler waved his keys at the soldiers. 'Yes, yes, release all the prisoners at once,' he commanded.

'And give me the key to the dungeon,' the Doctor requested, dabbing the sweat from his brow.

Obediently the gaoler handed it over.

'Thank you very much indeed,' the Doctor smiled, and turning on his heel, he strode away towards the dungeon where Susan still languished in total isolation, close to despair.

The rain dropped out of the hot black sky in great soaking blobs. Concealed in the porch opposite the prison, Barbara watched the laughing cheering throng of soldiers and deputies surge along the street and up to the gates of the *Conciergerie*. In their midst struggled the thin, crouched figure of Robespierre, his hands still cupped around his bloodily foaming mouth, and his elegant clothes covered in long trails of blood like streamers hanging from a maypole.

The leading soldier banged on the gates with his musket. 'Open up! We've got Robespierre! Open up for the Tyrant . . . ' he cried.

Barbara shuddered as the gates swung open and the crowd

pushed its way into the courtyard. She feared that the Doctor and Susan might find themselves trapped inside the *Conciergerie* in all the confusion. With Paris poised on a political knife-edge, nobody could feel safe now.

To her immense relief, Ian and James Stirling suddenly ran into the porch both soaked to the skin.

'Doctor not back yet?' Ian panted, anxiously eyeing the mass of citizens jamming the gates to the prison across the road.

Barbara shook her head. 'Robespierre's just been taken inside,' she murmured, still shocked by the memory. 'I saw him . . . It was horrible, Ian . . . '

Stirling leaned against the wall to recover his breath. 'Yes, we followed them here,' he gasped. 'Perhaps I should go in and find out what has happened to the Doctor . . . '

Ian grasped his arm firmly. 'You stay where you are!' he insisted. 'I don't think Citizen Lemaître would be very popular at the moment. Let's wait until Jules arrives with the transport.'

There was a tense pause while they watched the shoving, jostling crowd trying to force its way into the prison. Overhead, the thunderstorm flashed and hammered away, as if echoing the turbulent events taking place on the ground.

'I shall be making for Calais,' Stirling told them eventually. 'I can find a boat there.'

'Good, I think we can take you part of the way there,' Ian offered.

Stirling frowned at his two mysterious compatriots. 'I know absolutely nothing about you all . . . ' he exclaimed in a surprised voice, as if the fact had only just occurred to him. 'Where exactly are you heading?'

Before Ian could say too much, Barbara hastily intervened. 'Well, according to a map Jules showed us, we travel sort of north-west out of Paris . . . about fifteen kilometres,' she replied, sketching vaguely with her finger on the grimy window behind her.

Stirling looked even more puzzled than before. 'But I understood that you were . . . '

'Here's Jules!' Ian interrupted, as the clatter of hooves

and the rumble of wheels sounded suddenly above the racket in the sky.

The Doctor had been frantically struggling with the dungeon key, while the prison reverberated with the din of the storm and the clamour of newly-released prisoners and the arrival of Robespierre. At last the stiff lock snapped open and the Doctor strode into the smelly cell.

'Grandfather . . . Oh, Grandfather, is it really you at last?' Susan cried, collapsing into his arms, her face wet with tears.

'Yes, my child, it's all over now,' he murmured tenderly, hugging her and kissing her forehead. 'We're going straight back to the TARDIS,' he promised, leading Susan out of the dungeon and around the corner into the vault.

'Where are the others?' Susan asked weakly, leaning heavily on the Doctor's arm.

'Barbara is waiting in the street and Ian should be there too by now. Jules is bringing us a carriage,' the Doctor explained, hurrying her along.

Susan giggled nervously. 'Gosh, a carriage! We're certainly going to travel in style!' Her face suddenly froze as she saw the soldiers dragging the horribly wounded Robespierre down the steps at the other end of the vault. 'Grandfather, what's happening?' she exclaimed in a choked voice.

'They've arrested Robespierre,' the Doctor murmured, drawing Susan to one side where a group of freed prisoners were standing gazing around them in bewildered disbelief. 'You could call it a celebration,' he added ironically.

They watched the deposed tyrant being dragged over to the tipsy and equally bewildered gaoler in his alcove.

'Well, Citizen Robespierre, this is indeed an honour,' the gaoler chuckled, attempting a mock bow and staggering clumsily against his star prisoner.

'Don't waste your foul breath on him,' growled the leading militiaman. 'He can't answer you back. He tried to write us a letter. Too bad we can't read!'

A chorus of brutal jeers and raucous laughter erupted from the crowd thronging the steps.

'Let's go, my child,' murmured the Doctor, edging along

the wall towards the steps. 'The rabble are much too busy to bother about us. Yesterday they lived in fear of Robespierre. Today . . . '

The Doctor fell silent as he led Susan through the merciless crowd baying for revenge and ushered her swiftly out into the courtyard to safety.

Across the street from the prison gates a pair of horses waited patiently in the shafts of a four-wheeled enclosed carriage. Jules Renan had joined the others waiting apprehensively in the porch out of the torrential rain.

'Yes, the fall of Robespierre changes everything for us . . . ' Jules observed pensively.

Ian shrugged. 'I don't see why it should. People will still be arrested and condemned to the guillotine.'

'But our organisation was created to work against Robespierre,' Jules explained. 'We shall have to wait and see how his successors behave.'

'Barras will take over now of course,' Barbara said casually.

Jules shook his head doubtfully. 'I think he will be content to be commander of the military,' he replied. 'But Tallien will advance upwards.'

'And Fouché,' Barbara added.

Jules frowned. 'Yes, Fouché perhaps. And even Fréron . . . ' He suddenly smiled in surprise. 'You are extremely well informed about our ambitious politicians, Barbara. Who do you think will rule France eventually?'

Barbara smiled enigmatically. 'Eventually? Oh, none of those people, Jules. But remember the name of Napoleon Bonaparte . . . '

Jules stared at her in amused disbelief. 'A Corsican, ruler of France? Never!' he laughed in mock outrage.

James Stirling had been listening with intense interest. He would dearly have liked to discover more about the two young English persons and their mysterious friends. 'Now that I am at last going home I just cannot wait to see England again,' he confessed.

Barbara smiled secretively. 'Oh yes, I know exactly how you feel,' she agreed warmly. 'It's been such a long time.'

'Why not come with me?' Stirling suggested impulsively, hoping to prompt them to reveal more about their mysterious destination.

Ian shook his head emphatically. 'No, Stirling, we must go our own way,' he declared. 'I'm afraid you wouldn't understand.'

Before Stirling could pursue his curiosity, Ian suddenly caught sight of the Doctor leading Susan out of the gates of the *Conciergerie*. 'The Doctor! And he's got Susan!' he cried joyfully as they approached.

They all indulged in a brief but happy reunion, hugging, kissing, shaking hands and slapping one another on the back. Then Jules decided that it was time to leave. 'All of you into the coach . . . ' he ordered.

The driver, a trusted friend of Jules, opened the door and the Doctor bossily ushered Susan, Barbara and Ian inside before clambering in himself.

As the Doctor settled into a corner seat next to his granddaughter, a terrible shadow of anxiety passed across his face. Surreptitiously he felt in the pockets of his costume, his brow furrowing more and more deeply until his fingers at last closed around the key to the TARDIS. He *had* remembered to transfer it from his frock-coat in the tailor's shop after all!

For a moment or two, Jules and James Stirling were left alone in the porch. 'I hope they will have a safe journey,' Jules murmured.

'So do I,' Stirling agreed. 'But to *where*, Jules? It is strange, but I have the impression that they do not really know where they are going.' He paused and waved to the Doctor, who was beckoning to them out of the carriage window. 'But come to that, do any of us?' he grinned.

An hour later, after a hair-raising journey at break-neck speeds along the narrow rutted roads and after several last-minute detours to avoid flooded stretches and patrols combing the countryside for spies and saboteurs, the Doctor and his three companions took their leave of Jules Renan and James Stirling near the burnt-out farm. The sun was just appearing and the rain was petering out as they waved goodbye and the carriage clattered on its way towards

Calais. The air felt fresh and cool after the storm as they made their way on foot to the forest clearing where the TARDIS stood patiently among the branches.

Safely inside, the three younger travellers stood around the quietly humming control console, while the Doctor sat in his chair loosening the tight cravat and collar of his uncomfortable disguise. They were discussing whether or not their presence had exerted any real influence on the dramatic historical events of the past few days.

'I assure you, Barbara,' the Doctor was saying, 'Napoleon simply would not have believed you.'

'All right, Doctor,' Ian interrupted. 'Suppose one of us had written Napoleon a letter . . . you know, sort of describing some of the things that are going to happen to him . . .'

'It still wouldn't make any difference, Ian,' Susan argued. 'Napoleon would either lose it, or forget all about it, or decide it was written by a maniac.'

'And if we'd tried to shoot Napoleon, the bullet would have missed him,' Barbara mused thoughtfully.

The Doctor levered off his shoes and aired his stockinged feet gratefully. 'The mainstream of history is fixed and immutable,' he reminded them. 'I think you're all rather belittling the subject. Our own lives are important in themselves. To us, at present. As we experience things, so we learn.'

'But do we ever really learn anything?' Barbara wondered hopelessly.

'Of course we do,' Susan insisted earnestly. 'I mean, you and Ian aren't the same people who followed me home from school to the scrapyard in Totters Lane and forced your way into the TARDIS. You've both changed.'

Ian nodded ruefully. 'Yes, perhaps you're right,' he admitted, picking the Doctor's enormous plumed hat up from the console and plonking it on Susan's head. Susan looked much better now that the colour had returned to her face.

'Perhaps we've all changed,' Barbara said quietly.

'Well, I certainly intend to change out of this uncomfortable costume as soon as possible . . .' the Doctor announced, rising and approaching the console with a business-like air.

Ian looked at Barbara as if he was beginning to wish he had accepted James Stirling's invitation to accompany him to England after all. He would have ended up in the wrong century, but at least he would have had a pretty good chance of reaching the right location in space!

'So where to now, Doctor?' he asked nervously.

'Where to?' echoed the Doctor, throwing back his head and flaring his eager nostrils as if to sniff out a likely destination. He bent over the instruments and caught sight of the small circuit panel he had removed and left on the console three days before. He flexed his long fingers like a magician at a children's party and picked up the panel as if it were part of some fantastic conjuring trick.

'Who knows, Chesterton?' he chuckled drily, studying the dense circuitry with a roguish smile. 'Who knows? Because I certainly don't!'